"I TOLD YOU THIS WASN'T A GAME!"

"Then why didn't you let me in on this little scheme of yours? This is supposed to be a team effort."

"There's no such thing as team effort. Everyone is on his own, all alone in life. The sooner you know that, the better off you'll be."

Kelly stared, unable to believe her ears. Was this the man who'd held her in his arms, who'd spoken so tenderly to her? "You seem so open, but it's a lie, isn't it? Inside you're locked up, closed, too superior to share yourself with anyone."

"I don't need to share myself. I don't need anyone."

Kelly watched his jaw harden. He was like a rock—hard, unyielding, hurling himself against any emotional obstacle, shattering it like glass. "I wonder how many people you really fool," she said quietly, her eyes capturing his in a rare moment of naked truth.

He was the first to look away.

A CANDLELIGHT ECSTASY SUPREME

SHADOW GAMES

Elise Randolph

A CANDLELIGHT ECSTASY SUPREME

Published by
Dell Publishing Co., Inc.
1 Dag Hammarskjold Plaza
New York, New York 10017

Dell ® TM 681510, Dell Publishing Co., Inc.

Candlelight Ecstasy Supreme is a trademark of
Dell Publishing Co., Inc.

Candlelight Ecstasy Romance®, 1,203,540, is a registered
trademark of Dell Publishing Co., Inc.

ISBN: 0–440–17764–2

Printed in the United States of America
First printing—March 1984

To Our Readers:

Candlelight Ecstasy is delighted to announce the start of a brand-new series—Ecstasy Supremes! Now you can enjoy a romance series unlike all the others —longer and more exciting, filled with more passion, adventure, and intrigue—the stories you've been waiting for.

In months to come we look forward to presenting books by many of your favorite authors and the very finest work from new authors of romantic fiction as well. As always, we are striving to present the unique, absorbing love stories that you enjoy most—the very best love has to offer.

Breathtaking and unforgettable, Ecstasy Supremes will follow in the great romantic tradition you've come to expect *only* from Candlelight Ecstasy.

Your suggestions and comments are always welcome. Please let us hear from you.

Sincerely,

The Editors
Candlelight Romances
1 Dag Hammarskjold Plaza
New York, New York 10017

CHAPTER ONE

The migration had begun.

It happened every year about this time, as thousands of Americans went abroad. Like feathered fledglings, they would wing their way to new and distant lands, parading insolently through Europe and Asia. En masse, they would swoop down on an unsuspecting nation, preen and ruffle their red white and blue plumage, and troop bravely and irreverently past monuments and shrines that held no more significance to their lives than as possible backdrops for their photographs.

Kelly Milburn wanted no part in it.

She brushed her long brown hair back with

her hand and chuckled. "Asian Extravaganza! Oh, Ruth, I love it! This is a joke, right?"

"Afraid not, Kelly dear."

Kelly's chortles fizzled out and her eyes widened. "You're not kidding?"

The editor shook her head.

Kelly shifted her weight to her other slim hip and opened the leaflet with a solemn shake. She cleared her throat in official preparation for reading. "Frankfurt, Heidelburg, Delhi, Bombay, Bangkok, Hong Kong. And all of this in . . . let me see . . . ah, here it is. In fourteen days!"

She smiled sweetly at her editor. "Are they planning to travel at the speed of light?"

Ruth laughed, but stood her ground. "This is what you're being paid for. Look, Kelly, *Touring Magazine* is doing a whole issue on tours for the budget-minded. This fits right in."

"I've got a great idea!" Kelly grinned wickedly as the editor's assistant sashayed into the office. "Let's let Calvin handle it."

"I have him working on something else."

Kelly planted her hands on her waist and narrowed her eyes in suspicion. "What about my trip to Tanzania? I asked for the archeological dig near Olduvai Gorge."

Ruth deferred her answer by turning to readjust the blinds, shutting out the summer sun that glinted like luminous flames off the Chicago skyscape. She finally looked back at Kelly and shrugged. "That's what I have Calvin working on."

In her peripheral vision Kelly saw Calvin strut out of the office with his pointy little chin in the air. Incensed by this news, she engaged in a short, futile stare-down with Ruth, which the editor won simply by virtue of her status as boss.

Kelly made one last stab. "So this is it? I'm to spend two weeks on a geriatric tour?"

"Yes, dear, polyester and all. The tour leaves in three days. Please make sure you're on it. Oh, and by the way, you'd better take plenty of sunscreen to cover up that fair skin of yours. I understand India is deadly at this time of year."

"Great," Kelly grumbled, sighing over the predictability of her life. Did she ever get an exciting assignment? No. They all went to that little pinched-face weasel, Calvin. She walked out of the door, her insecurities making the doorway seem much larger than when she had walked into the room a few minutes ago.

She turned around one last time. "You know as well as I do that nothing exciting ever happens on these things."

Ruth smiled back. "Just think of it as paying your dues, my dear."

That's what I've been doing all my life, Kelly thought, but she didn't say so. "Right," she muttered instead.

Behind the desk Ruth shook her head. Even after three years, she couldn't understand Kelly. That girl was always looking for excitement, some elusive thrill. It seemed to her that a woman as vivacious as Kelly would have more excitement than she could handle. But then, life was full of its little mysteries.

Kelly closed her editor's door, grabbed her purse, and started home for the day, concentrating on all the things she would have to do before she left. She'd have to cancel her date for Friday night, but that certainly wouldn't break her heart . . . or his either. She'd have to get her neighbor to water her plants in the apartment, and take care of Harry, her Amazon parrot.

She also supposed she ought to call her mother and tell her where she was going. Although whether there would be any interest there or not was doubtful. But as always, she'd keep trying just in case.

She frowned as she thought of her parents. Ever since she was a young girl she had been seeking all the ways she could escape the suffocating memories of her childhood. Always searching for the means to thwart whatever fates might drag her back to the cruelty of her father or into a parallel existence with her mother.

There was a twisted irony to it all. For no matter how far from home she wandered or how many places she went looking for excitement and escape, she could not erase the fear of soul-degrading mediocrity and self-denying subservience that had plagued her since she was young.

Now all she had to look forward to was more of the same. Another run-of-the-mill tour. More mediocrity.

Kelly forcefully shoved away the threat of depression. She opened the door to her apartment and peered very cautiously around the opening in case Harry had gotten loose again. "Harry," she sang, "I'm home."

Bill Clayton opened the door to his apartment and, for only the slightest second, hesitated to enter.

The apartment was decorated in earth colors, browns and tweeds, but there was no warmth. There were no personal effects, no momentoes, no photographs, no signs of life. They had all been thrown into a box somewhere and shoved to the back of a closet.

Instead, it was the frozen study of a man

who had somehow lost time, or rather purposely left it behind, hiding from its effects, its memories, and its pain.

With a determined stride he crossed the threshhold and switched on his telephone answering machine to play back any messages. The present, that's where he was now. That's all that mattered.

He walked to the refrigerator and, as he moved, his blue nylon gym shorts and sleeveless T-shirt clung to the moisture that covered his well-toned body. Draping a terry-cloth towel around his neck, he poured a tall glass of orange juice and drank it in one gulp as he listened to the machine on the counter.

The University of Denver was calling to remind him that he had promised to speak to one of the business classes about international taxation and the foreign tax credit for U.S. corporations.

His stockbroker had a hot tip on Winthrop Oil.

Wharton University's alumni association was calling to invite him to this year's athletic awards ceremony. Due to his enduring school records in track, he would be an honorary guest. Could they count on his attendance at the ceremony?

There was a space on the machine where the next caller had hung up without leaving

14

a message. *Well, darn,* he thought facetiously. *I've probably missed another opportunity to discuss the merits of shampooing my carpets or buying more life insurance.*

And then there was the inevitable call from Lisa.

Bill gritted his teeth as he waited for the shrill accusations he knew would be forthcoming. "Where have you been, Bill Clayton? Why haven't you called me? It's been over a week. You knew how important it was to me for you to be there and watch me perform *Giselle* last weekend. I'm sick of it, Bill! You think you can treat women like dirt. No, not even that good. You treat women like . . ."

Blessedly, her invective was lost in the high beep that preceded the next message.

Bill flipped the machine off in agitation and ran his fingers through his damp sand-colored hair. He tried to push Lisa's message behind all other thoughts, but it edged forward, playing over and over again in his mind. He didn't want to admit that what she said was probably true. He just didn't want to face up to his own shortcomings right now.

He wiped his face with the towel and tossed it onto the couch, then walked to his desk and started opening the mail.

The first letter he opened was an ad for ranchettes in western Colorado, which he immediately crumpled and tossed into the trash, not even checking to see which great prize he might win by visiting the house sites and sitting through the sales pitch.

He picked up the next envelope and tore it open, staring with both curiosity and dismay at the announcement. It was a letter from Intercontinent Airlines informing him that he had been awarded the airline's seventy-five-thousand-mile prize.

Was this a joke? Whoever heard of a prize for flying on business trips? Still, he was a little surprised that he had been away from Denver that much this past year. The geophysics business was in another boom cycle, and his company now had land and marine crews operating all over the world. His job as vice-president of international finance and foreign taxation had forced him to travel. Go here, go there until . . . well, he'd apparently chalked up seventy-five thousand miles.

But he didn't want to win this trip. He'd had his share of prizes. It was funny in a strange sort of way how all the awards, trophies, scholarships, and honors had only spurred him further on his frustrating search for that indefinable thing that couldn't be won. The feeling of satisfaction continued to elude him.

His friends called him a workaholic, but he

wasn't. It was just that there had to be something you could attain or someplace you could reach where the past no longer mattered. That's all he really wanted.

He scanned the cover letter before pulling the full-color brochure from the envelope. Master Tours' Asian Extravaganza. *Give me a break!* he groaned. *After flying seventy-five thousand miles in one year on business, all I need is another trip!* Of course, he had never been on a trip just for fun. Ah, but then, who had time for fun?

Massaging the back of his tan neck to loosen the muscles that were still tense from a three-mile jog, he turned on the lamp beside the tweed couch. Shoving aside yesterday's *Wall Street Journal* and several business magazines, he sat down, stretching his long athletic legs out in front of him and propping his Adidas up on the coffee table.

He shook open the brochure from the airline and started to read. Frankfurt, Delhi . . . wild horses couldn't drag him on a trip like this. He didn't have the time.

. . . Bombay, Bangkok, Hong Kong. Bangkok. He thought about some of his Vietnam veteran friends and their sizzling tales of R & R in Thailand. Something about a special body massage. Hmm, perhaps this trip could be a socially and culturally redeeming experience.

Bill's daydream was interrupted as the door to his bedroom opened and a willowy young woman walked out into the living room. He turned and looked at her, trying very hard not to wish she were not here, wearing his bathrobe. But he did wish that. He hardly knew this woman in any other than the physical sense and he really wasn't sure he wanted to know her any better.

She bent over the back of the couch, her blond hair falling into Bill's upturned face, and the robe flared open at the neck. She pouted effectively. "Do you always run out like that on a girl in the morning?"

He stared at her exposed throat and the soft white curves of her breasts, then fought to suppress his body's immediate reaction.

Was this the only type of relationship he had to look forward to in his life? Surely there was something more. "I exercise every morning," he said. "Have to keep in shape." He knew he sounded harsh and brusque, but he couldn't force feelings for her that he didn't have. Damn, he hated himself at times like this.

The woman moved around the couch and stood before the man she had met only last night. "I like to exercise in the morning too," she purred seductively as her eyes traveled down the length of his body. "Why don't we exercise together?"

Bill's face was unmoving as he watched her sway back into the bedroom, turn and smile, then quietly close the door. Leaning his head back against the couch, he puffed out his cheeks and expelled a spiritless breath of air. He had been holding it in since she first bent over the couch.

Why was it always like this? He wanted a woman he could like and respect. So why did he end up with women he didn't care about at all? Was it him? Was he too lazy, too superficial, too cold? Just once he'd like to have a real relationship. Just once he'd like to find someone he could trust, believe in.

He looked back at the brochure still clutched in his hand, attempting to mentally shift gears and turn his mind from the woman in his bedroom.

They certainly would be shocked at his company if he just walked in and said, "In three days I'm leaving on vacation." Bill Clayton simply wasn't that spontaneous. And he never took his three weeks of allotted vacation time. What was the point? There was nothing worthwhile to do with it anyway.

He heard the woman turn on the shower tap. The sound of the water fell in a rhythmic cascade through the wall, hypnotizing him. Bill gazed around the too tidy apartment, not seeing the loneliness, aware only of the emptiness.

He didn't need a vacation any more than he needed that woman in his shower. But something . . . he needed something. "Damn! What the hell's the matter with me?"

He stood up, dropping the brochure onto the floor, and walked across the room. He hated doubt and indecision. They were the product of a weak man. Bill Clayton would never be a weak man. No, he had to get rid of the doubts.

The hypnotic sound of running water beckoned him as he walked into the bedroom, pulled the T-shirt off over his head, and tossed it into the laundry hamper. He entered the bathroom, pulled back the shower curtain, and smiled as he watched the woman run the bar of soap across her body. But there was a wistful sadness in the smile. And he wondered if, like him, she ever wanted more than this.

Miles away in Dallas, vacation was the last thing on George Watterman's mind. In a weak moment of frustration he collapsed into the large brown suede chair at the head of the conference table. His breath was no more than a shallow and uneven pant.

Take it easy. That's what that fresh young kid who had the nerve to call himself a doctor was always saying. *You're not a young man anymore.* Hell, what did that punk know about it? He was barely out of diapers himself.

And then there was Virginia and her infernal nagging. *You're going to kill yourself! Think about me for a change! Think what will happen to me if you die!*

God, they all made him sick.

But he had shown them. Shown them all. He had what it took. He didn't have the fancy education. But he had the guts and the know-how it took to build this empire. Damn it all, George Watterman was no loser!

Drawing on a seemingly inexhaustible reservoir of strength and bull-headed stubbornness, George loosened his tie and stood once again to face the men around the table, the dark distended veins in his face pulsating with rage.

"How in the name of heaven could this have happened! How!"

"Had to have been an inside job," one of the senior vice-presidents offered unconvincingly. "Someone in data processing maybe?"

This time the whey-faced vice-president of new development spoke up. "How the heck would anyone in processing know about this project? If it was an inside job, it has to have been someone close to the research operation itself. Someone in Frankfurt who was involved from the beginning."

George Watterman walked away from the table in an effort to control his anger, and ran his huge hand along the smooth, paneled wall of the boardroom. He had been president of Lambert Technologies for fourteen years and had been working for the company since he was eighteen. He hadn't been hired like one of those know-it-all college boys. He had been hired to work.

He had begun his career in the field, working first on seismic vessels, then moving on to the oil fields as a roughneck, and later working on contracts for the U.S. Defense Department. He was even the first one to come up with the idea of using computers in military surveillance planes. It sure as hell wasn't one of these Ivy League hotshots who thought of that. It was him, George Watterman, high school dropout.

He turned around and stared pointedly at his vice-presidents sitting around the table waiting for direction and guidance. Damn! Couldn't they think for themselves?

"I don't care which one of your departments is responsible," George spoke softly, menacingly, to his underlings. "If I don't get that computer chip back, you're all going to pay out the ass for this."

His gaze jumped to the man at the end of the table. "Where do we start, Jake?"

"Frankfurt." The chief security officer for Lambert Technologies, Jake Balletoni, leaned back in the plush chair, his hands clasped behind his head. He took a long drag on his cigar, expelling a warm yellow cloud of smoke that circled lazily about his head before drifting down the table to the others.

He spoke without removing the cigar from between his clenched teeth. "We start with each department. We find the bastards. Then we squeeze them dry."

The other executives squirmed in their chairs, trying to curb their uneasiness. Composed and indifferent, Jake Balletoni slipped the cigar to the other side of his mouth using only his tongue, lips, and teeth.

The only one in the room who didn't seem concerned with the security officer's lack of diplomatic euphemisms was George Watterman. He and Jake went back a long, long time together. They had flown a decrepit Piper Cub out of Peru during the coup sixteen years ago. They had worked side by side in the jungles of Ecuador and in the deserts of Bahrain. Together they had experienced and escaped hell.

Jake was the man for this job. There was none better.

"There's been no ransom call or letter," George pointed out. "So some other company has to be paying for it. I want to know that too."

"You'll have all the answers," Jake said with a pragmatic nod.

One of the vice-presidents cleared his throat, then asked reluctantly the question that was on everyone's mind. "What will you do with the culprit who has the computer chip once you find him?"

Slipping the cigar to the other side of his mouth again, Jake stared at the man who had asked the question. He never uttered a word.

Through the plume of yellow smoke his unblinking black eyes said it all.

CHAPTER TWO

Kelly shifted the flight bag to her other hand. With each passing minute that Flight 102 to Frankfurt was delayed, the bag gained extra pounds, its weight growing in direct proportion to her exasperation with this whole escapade. Looking for an empty chair, she threaded her way through Master Tours' restless group of travelers who had gathered in the lobby of J.F.K. to wait for their plane.

Her attention was drawn momentarily to Mr. Fowler, a barrel-chested man whose military bearing rivaled that of General Patton. While straightening his ill-fitting toupee, he delivered a lengthy diatribe on American foreign policy to Mrs. Willard and her teenage niece, Muffy.

"It can be put in terms that, if you'll excuse me, even you ladies will understand. America has the might. If those pansies in Washington would just pull their heads out of their"—he cleared his throat and readjusted the hairpiece—"the sand, they'd see that. Hell, we don't have to listen to what France wants or what West Germany wants. We just bring in the damn missiles and plant them in their backyards. It's as simple as that."

Mrs. Willard, awe-inspired, was nodding at the man's sage evaluation of American diplomacy. Muffy stood beside her, popping gum and mumbling uninterested "Fer shurrr's."

Kelly pursed her lips. *My sentiments exactly, Muffy*. She observed them quietly for a long moment, making mental notes of each eccentricity for her article before turning her attention to some of the other passengers. A cloud of cigar smoke attacked her nose and eyes and her gaze swung to a stocky, dark-eyed man leaning nonchalantly against the wall. For the split second that their eyes met and held, she felt a strange ribbon of uneasiness curl through her stomach. She sincerely hoped she wouldn't have to sit next to him on the plane.

26

She turned away and continued walking down the aisle between the chairs. Just ahead, the Parkers, an attractive couple who bore the unmistakable stamp of suburban life, wrestled with their two hyperactive children, alternately bribing and castigating them in a futile attempt to modify their behavior.

An elderly white-haired man, wearing hiking boots and a tweed jacket over a Peruvian llama sweater, winked and tipped his Eddie Bauer hat to Kelly as she walked past. She smiled back and took a seat in a gray, contoured plastic chair that was bolted to the airport floor, arranging her purse and travel bag around her ankles, and retying the sleeves of her cardigan sweater around her shoulders.

A sweet-looking old couple seated next to her was involved in an intimate conversation over their belongings, shuffling and rearranging their small bags and camera cases. Their effortless dialogue with each other carried a mellow harmony found only in marriages that have already been through the bad times and somehow survived them all.

The quick rising of Kelly's eyebrow was the only sign of her skepticism. The only marriage she had observed close at hand was her parents', and it had died before the bad times even started.

What an odd melange of people, she mused

as she surveyed the motley group of travelers with whom she would be spending the next fourteen days. Fatalistically resigned to the task of chronicling this particular pilgrimage for *Touring Magazine,* Kelly was still far from delighted about it. Who cared what types of people signed up for these fast-paced tours? Her readers would be as bored as she was.

Already kicking himself for signing up for this ridiculous trip, Bill Clayton let his eyes scan the group with whom he was to travel. One man, sitting three chairs away, had a long, thin neck and a weak chin and bore an uncanny resemblance to E.T. And those three elderly ladies next to him hadn't stopped babbling since they sat down.

"I just can't *wait* to see the Taj Mahal," Edna Blumberg squealed and clutched her pocketbook to her breast.

"I don't know," Pearl Henshaw shook her head, lowering her voice to emphasize the enormity of her suspicions. "I hear that country is so dirty. I certainly hope I don't catch the plague or anything."

"Well," Leona Miller chirped brightly. "I'm looking for some real bargains when we get to Bangkok. I promised my daughter and granddaughter that I'd bring them something nice from the Orient. I was thinking about one of

28

those cute little carved Buddhas with the fat tummies. What do you think?"

Bill closed his eyes and cursed himself for succumbing to spontaneity. So, he'd won the trip. He didn't have to take the damn thing. It had been one of the few times in his life when he'd acted without really thinking. It was some crazy need for change or something. Heaven help him if he were going through a midlife crisis at thirty-four! Too bad the airline wasn't just giving away the money instead of the trip. Spending a couple of weeks with the three merry widows wasn't exactly his idea of fun.

Of course, the trip wasn't going to be all play. He always tried to combine some business with pleasure—it was more *efficient*. He was not comfortable indulging himself strictly in pleasure. He had made that his motto before most of his friends even knew the meaning of work. And it was one of the reasons he had been so successful all his life in sports, in school, and in his profession.

So as long as he was going to this side of the world, he would take care of business too. He glanced down beside his feet at the briefcase full of computer circuit boards, his mind now full of the technicalities of the geophysics industry.

It was the slim, red-tipped toes under the

strap of a sandal that first caught his attention and shot a quick, pleasurable spark through his body. All thoughts of work immediately retired to the back of his mind.

His eyes rose to follow her swaying hips as Kelly passed by and took a seat across and farther down from him. Without expression he studied her as she set her purse and flight bag at her feet and watched with interest as she began to candidly inspect the rest of the group assembled in the departure lounge.

She had a very pretty face, strong and somewhat haughty. Her cheekbones were high and her nose was sharply defined, but it was her mouth that captured his attention. She held it in a tight line of detached amusement, setting herself apart from all of this with a kind of bored resignation.

Bill stretched his legs out in front of him and crossed his arms. His gaze slid down her body in slow perusal, a little disappointed that the curves and angles were mostly hidden from view by her stylishly loose trousers, large cotton shirt, and cardigan sweater tied around her shoulders.

When his eyes rose once again to her face, he saw that she was looking at him, holding her mouth and eyes in an undeviating pose that was as cool and superior as that of a Roman goddess.

Kelly didn't take her eyes off the man who had been staring at her for several minutes. She couldn't. His eyes were so starkly penetrating it was as if he were mentally undressing her. The very idea produced goose flesh all over her body. But she refused to look away from him. If he wanted a staring contest, she was ready for it. Still, her flesh prickled and stung from the sensual images his eyes invoked. Who was he anyway?

Yesterday she had studied the passenger roster carefully to get an idea of who was going on this tour. So she figured he could be one of two men. Bill Clayton, the accountant, or Damien Brewster, the life insurance salesman.

She attempted to study him with the same casual indifference he was using on her. He had long legs under khaki slacks, muscular arms beneath an Oxford-cloth shirt, and large, well-sculpted hands that rested on the arms of the chair.

His hair was the color of the beach on a soft summer evening. His skin was ruddy and bronze, his features classic and well-proportioned. She wasn't close enough to determine the color of his eyes, but they were dark and demanding—that much she could tell.

It was hard to tell. He could be either one of the men. But he looked so athletic—not what she'd expect from a man with a desk job. And he seemed so cool, so arrogant. She finally shifted her eyes away from him. No way did she need a man like that in her life—even if he was gorgeous. She needed excitement, something to drive away the ennui of this tour, but she didn't need disaster.

She didn't really know what kind of man she was most attracted to, but she had no doubts about what kind she didn't want. Her father had taken care of that decision for her. The memory of his growling voice was like an incantation exorcising any doubts she'd ever had on that subject. "I'm home now and I expect you to be quiet and keep out of my way." The grip of his fingers would tighten almost unbearably on her arm and her mother would silently turn her head toward the window. "I don't want to know you're here," he would yell. "You got that?"

Kelly swallowed hard, pushing the memories down, down, into the depths of her soul. Yes, she got it all right. She had been running away from it for twenty-nine years. And she was going to make sure that an attraction for the wrong type of man did not drag her back.

Bill's eyes narrowed a little as he watched her gaze shift away from him. Her critical scrutiny of him had amused him. She probably thought he was attracted to her. Hah! All he was doing was sizing up the people he would be traveling with. That's all.' There were beautiful women all over the world. This one was nothing special.

He refused to give credence to the coil of electricity that sparked to life inside his body. It was just a physical reaction, nothing unusual. Besides, this woman looked like she would demand too much attention. He didn't have time for more than a holiday fling.

He suddenly thought of what Lisa had said about him. That he treated women like dirt. No, even worse than that. Damn, this was supposed to be a vacation. Enough of this self-analysis!

He looked back at Kelly in time to see a thin man dressed in tight black slacks and a silk shirt unbuttoned to the waist stop in front of her. The man leaned down toward her and the heavy gold medallions around his neck swung precariously in her face. Bill couldn't tell what was being discussed because her expression never changed. But when the man stood up and turned around, his face wore the expression of a sprinter who had been knocked down in mid-stride.

Rejected but still cool, Damien Brewster swept his right hand back across his slick hair and sauntered on down the row, surveying the territory for another target for his affections.

Kelly checked off the name in her mind. Well, at least now she knew which one was the accountant and which one the salesman. She glanced back at Bill and their eyes locked for one brief instant in a flickering stare that gave no clue to what either of them was thinking. And yet, she was left feeling weak and vulnerable from the moment of visual contact. Flustered, she looked away.

Just then the tour director stood before the group in her too tight, too short skirt and announced that it was time to board the plane. "I know you are all going to just have a marvelous time. Mar-ve-lous!" As everyone gathered their belongings and began the slow push toward the waiting plane, Bill wondered whom the director was trying to convince, herself or them.

"Now, your tour guide will meet you as you disembark in Frankfurt," she continued in her frothy, effervescent voice. "You are just going to love the little man, and I can't wait to hear all about your exciting little adventures when you come home. Bon voyage, my little world travelers!"

"God! I feel like I'm in Munchkin land," Kelly muttered to no one in particular as she passed within inches of Bill.

A subtle tightening gripped his lower body when he first heard her low, seductive drawl. He chuckled at the remark and watched her walk on ahead, wondering if perhaps he had been too hasty in squelching his reaction to her. After all, there was certainly nothing wrong with having a light summer romance.

Shrugging away the notion, he picked up his briefcase full of microchip circuit boards and was herded with the others onto the late afternoon flight to Germany.

Jake Balletoni shifted his leather jacket to his left arm and waited until all the other passengers were out of the way. He hated crowds. For that matter, he hated air travel too. By boat—now, that was the way to go, feeling both the shift of the earth and the drag of the moon as the waves tossed the vessel upon the water. The sea. To this day he could feel it in his bones.

Miguel Andria Balletoni was born in Paola, a small village south of Naples on the Tyrrhenian Sea. The son of a dockworker, Miguel left home at seventeen, migrating south and finally crossing the Strait of Messina and settling in Palermo. Within a month of his arrival in Sicily, he had joined the crew of a fishing vessel, and there he learned the ancient, sometimes ruthless codes of manhood and survival. After two years he began to think that he had learned it all. Little did he know he had hardly begun.

Shortly after his nineteenth birthday, the fishing vessel sailed into the Aegean, stopping first at Mikonos and two days later docking in port at Athens. After the boat's catch was sold to the highest bidder, Miguel disembarked with the rest of the crew for a night of bacchanalian revelry.

It was noon the next day before he woke up. He was lying in a place he didn't recognize, hung over, bruised, and penniless. It must have been that faceless woman he had been with the night before. He touched the painful contusion on his side. But who had beaten him so badly? He lay back in the grass, drained. His memory was completely obliterated by the alcohol.

When he finally made his way back to the dock, the boat had sailed. The crew with whom he'd spent the last two years had returned to Sicily without him.

Without enough money for either booze or women, Miguel quickly grew restless. When a ship owned by the American company, Lambert Technologies, docked in port with the intention of signing on able men, Miguel Andria Balletoni was first in line.

Within a few weeks Jake Balletoni, as he

was now known, caught the attention of George Watterman, the coordinator on the seismic vessel. The two men liked each other instantly. Days of hard work and nights of revelry strengthened the bond between them. One night, after George drank the better part of a fifth of a particular type of whiskey known to the crew only as gutter sludge, he mentioned to Jake that a young Athenian woman he had been seeing for some time was attempting to blackmail him, threatening to show his wife certain compromising photographs if he didn't surrender a small fortune. George had no intention of paying her one red cent and yet he didn't know what in hell he was going to do about it.

Several days after this confession, George learned that Jake Balletoni had taken care of the situation. He never asked how. His friend had simply handled it.

It was the first of many instances that tied the two men together in a kind of symbiotic relationship. And others with the company learned to depend on Jake to bail them out of trouble as well.

When four geologists were taken hostage by an insurgent band of M-19 guerrilla soldiers in the Putumayan region of Colombia, Jake was the one who devised and orchestrated the successful operation that freed them.

Flying a helicopter kamikaze-style into the group of soldiers, and toting a stolen Russian AK-47 rifle, he single-handedly rescued the four men and flew them safely out of the region.

Twenty years later, when George brought him in as head of security for Lambert Technologies, Jake followed the same unbending precepts that had been laid down to him at seventeen.

Whoever tangled with Jake Balletoni had better be ready to pay the price.

He now sniffed disdainfully at the fat silver jet that was expelling black smoke outside the window. At the last minute he stubbed out his cigar in the ashtray and walked down the concourse onto Flight 102 to Frankfurt.

CHAPTER THREE

Two jolting sensations heralded Kelly's arrival in Germany. But while one was merely irritating, the other was physically devastating. Damien Brewster inspired the irritation when, in a flurry of impatience to be the first one in line for customs inspection, he whizzed past her, knocking her literally off her feet.

But it was the feel of Bill Clayton's strength under her arms, wrapping her like a steel band across her breasts, that completely devastated her. She was leaning back against his chest; his hand that held his briefcase was stretched across the front of her thighs.

Even after she had regained her balance, it

seemed he had held her much too long. She finally freed herself from his grasp, hoping the flush of her cheeks wasn't as evident to him as it was to her.

"Thank you." She tried to smile politely, forcing her gaze away from the dark blue of his eyes. She had known they were dark, but she hadn't expected them to be blue. It was the muted color, as if some shade had been drawn over them to hide whatever thoughts or emotions lay beneath, that had deceived her.

He, too, looked away. "Don't mention it."

They both continued their trek to immigration, neither speaking, but both very aware of each other's presence.

Well, all right, Kelly, get out of this situation as gracefully as possible. Be nice to the man and then send him on his way. "My name's Kelly Milburn."

He studied her a minute, looking as if he were trying to deduce some ulterior motive for the statement. His expression made her very uncomfortable. "Bill Clayton," he finally said.

She liked the sound of his voice. It was deep and resonant, but she immediately squelched the alarming sensation it awakened in her. For self-protection she wrapped a supercilious cloak around herself and heard the reflection of it in her voice. "It was my mother's name."

"Your mother's name was Bill?"

"No . . . no." She laughed self-consciously. "Kelly." *God, how stupid I sound! Who cares, anyway? Why in heaven's name are you rattling on this way?* "Actually it was her professional name. Her name was Eugenia Kelly Jameson. She hated the name Eugenia."

Why was she telling him all this? She sounded so nervous. Did he frighten her? he wondered. Maybe he should reciprocate and tell her all about his mother and father too. That would really scare her away. His mouth tightened as his mother's voice rang stridently through his mind. "You're a loser! Just like your father. You're no good. You'll never be."

He clenched his jaw as if he could squeeze the hurt out of old wounds that never healed. He focused on Kelly's remark to pull him out of the past. "What was she, an actress or something?"

"Singer. Opera singer."

"Really? It must have been exciting growing up with a professional singer."

Kelly stared at Bill for a frozen moment, wondering what she could possibly say to that. He had actually sounded sincere. Exciting? She thought about the different stages of her life. The needs, the wants, that were never fulfilled. But she couldn't talk about that with a stranger.

"Painfully," she answered.

His frown was imperceptible. Painfully! What a weird thing to say. Her smile was wide, but there was something a little too bright in her eyes, too crisp in her voice. He caught it all, but he didn't want to dwell on it too much.

Forget it, Bill. She's gorgeous to look at, but don't show too much interest. She might get the mistaken impression that you want to get involved with her.

"Well, nice talking to you," he said, quickening his stride to move on ahead into the customs line. "See you later."

Kelly felt the spirit within her deflate as Bill Clayton walked on ahead. But then, she wasn't interested in him anyway. Not really. A spiral of heat snaked through her body, setting the lie aflame. Okay, so he was very nice-looking, especially up close, and his arms, when they had wrapped around her body, were strong and sure and warm. But there was something cold and closed about him. It was almost as if he were angry at her for some reason. But what had she done wrong?

That was the one question she had been asking herself all her life.

Pull yourself together, girl. There are

enough crazies on this tour without you add-ing to the number. As if to confirm that fact, Leona Miller fluttered around the waiting room like a hysterical overstuffed peacock that had just lost its feathers.

"But my suitcase is so easy to identify!" she squawked. "It's pink, and I have some yarn tassels hanging on the handle so that I can spot it before anyone else does. I know how these airports are. I hear there are people who hang around the conveyor belts just waiting to grab the prettiest bag they can find. I knew I should have brought that old portmanteau my husband used during the war. I knew it!"

The brightly colored woven band of Kelly's thirty-five millimeter camera hung conve-niently around her neck. She removed the lens cap and, focusing on Leona Miller and a much smaller customs official, captured the woman in the very act of gobbling up the most unfortunate man.

Kelly noticed an old woman with a black scarf tied tightly against her head sitting on a bench against the wall on the other side of the room. She was perched on the very end, as if she were afraid she might take too much room on the bench. But she was crowding no one; there was no one else sitting there.

Kelly recognized the look on her face,

knew the essence of it, and she focused the lens to capture the expression. She clicked the shutter, then lowered the camera slowly.

From his own position in the long line, Bill was watching Kelly. He was trying to look detached, but he couldn't control the puzzled frown that creased his forehead when he followed her line of vision to the old woman on the bench.

He watched Kelly as she finished taking the picture. Her eyes held a drained look, an emptiness that was at odds with the vitality she projected a while ago. He stared at her for a long time, aware of a warm feeling coursing through his body. When he realized it was due to more than physical desire, he forcefully shook the sensation away. *Whatever you're thinking,* he told himself, *forget it. Keep this up and you're heading straight for a lobotomy.*

Utter pandemonium reigned in the Frankfurt airport. As one of the hubs of international travel, there was a mass of humanity —tourists, soldiers, children—all with at least two pieces of luggage en route to some outer point of the European wheel.

Jake Balletoni hoped the only other plane he would have to get on again would be the one back to the States. He followed the rest of

44

the passengers to customs. He was impatient to be in downtown Frankfurt, probing Lambert's research and development plant where the computer chip had been stolen.

The ratio of the chip's importance to its size was something he had trouble comprehending. A silver-gray fleck was all it was. And yet George had intimated that it could revolutionize society. How could one side of a quarter-inch flake of silicon hold a million electronic components? Units of information measured in Ks, very large-scale integration transistors, electrical signals that traveled at nearly the speed of light, were scientific wonders that Jake had not the background nor basis to understand.

He was aware that, after oxygen, silicon was the most abundant element on earth. And that there was something about the element's properties that could be altered to create electronic switches on transistors that controlled electrical signals. After that he was lost.

He did know that Lambert had been working on the design for this new chip since last June. Only a few key people knew about the highly secret project. Until three days ago Jake had not been one of those key people. George and a few of his top computer engineers had sweated for over a year on its development.

Computer research and development was a competitive field filled with constant fear that some other firm or some other country would get to the marketplace first with the newest and most advanced development in computer technology.

Even the U.S. Defense Department worried that America was falling behind, that the United States would grow dangerously dependent on foreign memory chips for its telecommunications satellites and advanced weaponry.

In California's silicon valley, industrial heists of computer chips were becoming commonplace. Stolen designs for parallel processors and VLSI circuits were worth millions of dollars in research and development costs to corporations or even nations that needed the advanced technology so badly they would steal for it. Anyone with the right knowledge and equipment could walk into any store and buy complex American chips off the shelf, make detailed photographs of them, and then copy the design layout. Or, carrying only what could fit in the palm of a hand or a pants cuff, someone could walk out of a laboratory or assembly plant with a fortune in new technology.

But a theft like this had never happened at Lambert before. It had certainly never happened since Jake was in charge of security. In his mind, it was a personal attack. And he would not rest until the chip was safely back in the lap of Lambert Technologies. The unwritten code had been ingrained in him for too many years. He would not relent until the job was done.

Standing in the customs line now, he watched a man being questioned thoroughly by officials. He was in the next aisle over, so Jake couldn't hear what was being said. But the young man's briefcase was open and a whole array of computer circuitry was in view. Jake's eyes widened. A veritable hardware store of electronic devices!

Bill snapped the lid on his briefcase shut and walked over to join the tour group already clustered in one corner of the lobby. It had taken him longer to pass inspection than it had the others because of all the electronic equipment he was carrying. He might as well get used to it. Until he was able to drop off the stuff at the office in Bangkok, he was going to have to fight his way through customs in Delhi and Bombay.

The geophysical crew made up of juggies, observers, drillers, and surveyors in Thailand needed the computer hardware by next week and hand-carrying it was the only reliable way of getting equipment like this to remote locations on the other side of the world.

He edged into the circle of tourists, between Bernard ("E.T.") Evanston, Ph.D., a philosophy professor from Iowa State University and Winfred Rotterborg, who dressed more like an Alpine mountain climber than a dentist from Salt Lake City.

The little man who was to escort the group on their trip was standing in the middle of the circle, his hands clasped in a prayerlike posture and his smile stretched beyond the outermost bounds of enthusiasm.

"My name is Lapito Ruta Migada Angelique. I be your guide tru Germany, India, Thailand, and Hong Kong."

Gauging his own reaction to the man against the reactions of the people around him, Bill concluded that the guide was going to be a royal pain in the rear.

His nationality was indeterminable and his English almost unintelligible. Though he claimed to be from Guinea, he could just as easily have been from Turkey or Portugal or Tibet or Timbuktu.

"We going to be in deluxe hotel," he tittered, his dark eyes flashing with self-absorbed amusement. "That mean it come with french fries." His high-pitched laugh bounded off the perimeter of the circle, returning to him in a solemn echo of weary sighs.

Already fatigue and jet lag had settled upon the group. Bill had been forced the entire flight from New York to listen to Indian chants from the glassy-eyed youth next to him and to fend off repeated attempts to convert him to Hare Krishna. He was certainly not in the mood for a guide who thought he was Bob Hope.

"Now!" The little man clapped his hands to signal everyone's attention. "I go find carts for our bugs."

"Bugs!" Fifteen-year-old Muffy slurred in her pinched nasal drawl.

"Yes," the guide nodded. "You have bugs, no?"

The young girl huffed indignantly. "No, I don't have bugs! I mean, like I'm sure. How gross!"

Lapito Ruta Migada Angelique's eyes darted about in agitation. "But, then . . . where are your clothes?"

"In my bag."

"That's what I say. In your bug."

Muffy rolled her eyes and snapped her gum.

"Now, I be back in"—Angelique stared at his watch for a good ten seconds—"four and a half minutes."

Bill tried to suppress a groan. What was he doing here? What had he signed up for? How was he ever going to keep himself sane for the next two weeks?

Standing back from the flow of passengers, Jake's attention was riveted on the small dark man who walked away from the tour group that had been on his flight. What was he supposed to be, some sort of guide? Jake's gaze followed him as he wove through the crowd in search of available luggage carts.

But it was the two men he passed, one blond and the other redheaded, that drew Jake's attention. Dawson and Kleinman—two of the top computer engineers at Lambert. What were they doing here in the airport?

As if on some prearranged cue, they began moving steadily toward the tour group. They stopped in front of the man who had carried the briefcase of computer hardware through customs. Jake smiled at the unexpected gift, leaned back against the wall, and watched the three men's every move.

"Bill Clayton?"

"Yeah?"

The blond spoke for both men. "We're with Lambert in Frankfurt. I'm Edgar Dawson and this is Klaus Kleinman." They pulled out company identification badges and showed them to Bill. "We heard from Worldwide that you were coming through here. Someone in your department said you were on vacation."

"Afraid so. Although I may go crazy with all this leisure time on my hands."

Dawson chuckled. "Well, maybe we can help you out with that problem. Actually, orders came down from above to get a computer chip to New Delhi as quickly as possible. Our boss said to check with Worldwide and see if anyone in the company was going that way. When we found out you were, we thought we would try to intercept you here in the airport."

"What is it?" Bill asked.

"Oh, it's just a chip that goes to our office there . . . for one of the in-house computers. We would have someone from our office take it, but everyone is tied up right now with other projects. And since we heard that you were already carrying electronic hardware to Bangkok for Worldwide, we hoped you wouldn't mind dropping off this in Delhi while you are there."

Bill shrugged. "I suppose not." Lambert Technologies used to do all its own geophysical work until it took over the smaller company, Worldwide Geophysical. And since it was now one of Lambert's most profitable subsidiaries, the parent company kept a tight rein over Worldwide's finances and its employees. "Does it go to the Lambert office there?"

"Ah, well . . . yes." Dawson, the blond man, answered hesitantly. "However, the man you'll be giving it to is named Fritz Graber." He handed Bill a business card with Fritz's name and address on it. "Please call him at this number as soon as you get to your hotel. You'll be staying at the Oberoi?"

Bill checked the itinerary in his pocket. "Yes, but I'll just drop it at the office as soon as I get there."

"There's no need." The redhead insisted. "Fritz will talk to you about it further if you will just call him. We don't want to inconvenience you more than necessary."

Bill's eyes narrowed on the man, then shifted to the other. He took the ceramic case that protected the tiny fleck of silicon from the blond man and slipped it into his briefcase. He looked at the business card before storing it away in his pocket. "It's no inconvenience. As you say, I've got others in here. What's one more?"

Jamming an unlit cigar into his mouth, Jake noted every detail about the young man to whom they had given what appeared to be a protective case for computer chips. It was the same man who only moments before had displayed to the customs official a briefcase full of computer hardware.

Slowly and thoughtfully, Jake struck a match against the textured wall and held the flame to the end of the cigar, one eye closing against the sulphur-laden smoke that drifted upward. He dropped the extinguished match onto the floor and nodded his head. "I'll be goddamned."

CHAPTER FOUR

It was an intuitive thrust in his gut combined with a prickling sensation along the back of his neck that made Bill turn around and stare.

He worked at keeping his expression blank as his eyes locked with those of a man standing about twenty feet away. Dark hair, stocky build, Italian or maybe Greek. Mediterranean. Black eyes that burned a hole right through the cigar smoke that circled about his head.

Paranoia, Bill. That's all it is. That guy's not really looking at you. Instinctively, he placed a protective hand over the pocket of his Oxford-cloth shirt, feeling the soft, worn contours of his passport. The guy might be someone who wanted safe passage to the States, but couldn't get a passport or visa. That was always a possibility. A photograph was easy enough to change and signatures could be forged. It happened all the time. Yes, that was probably it. The man was after his papers.

He expelled a sigh of relief and felt the tension ebb from his body. There were very few problems over which he didn't have dominion. Control was his forte. So, whatever this guy's problem was, he could handle it.

The guide returned and doled out the luggage carts as if the travelers were schoolchildren receiving their lunches. They would be spending the day and night in Frankfurt, then tomorrow they were going by train to Heidelburg for the day before returning to Frankfurt tomorrow night.

Kelly made a wry face in response to that thought. Obviously that was Master Tours' idea of a visit to Germany.

The two Parker brats were now dragging her soft-sided suitcase around the floor and straddling it like a horse. After a few well-placed threats, she was able to retrieve it and heave it up onto her luggage cart.

The three elderly women from Oklahoma were having trouble with their baggage, but before Kelly could assist them Mr. Fowler came to their aid, magnanimously offering both his services and his imperious maxims on the need for a strong military defense.

Lapito Ruta Migada Angelique made a complete fool of himself and embarrassed the entire tour group by marching his little charges through the airport like a scout troop, then stomping up to the front desk of the Sheraton Hotel, which was connected to the airport terminal by a covered bridge, and demanding VIP service for them.

Hans Ziegfried, the unfortunate desk clerk on duty, instantly forced an obligatory smile to greet the noisy Americans. "*Guten Morgen.* Good morning. If you will stand in line for just one moment, we will have you all in your rooms in no time at all."

Fowler, puffed up in his General Patton impression, shoved his way to the front of the line. "Where can I buy some of them German dollars?"

Hans cleared his throat. "Deutsche Marks, Mr. . . ."

"Fowler."

"Ah, of course," Hans replied smoothly and took a deep breath. "After you are registered, the cashier will be happy to exchange your money."

"Well, he better not issue me too many of

them dooooch marks," Fowler grumbled. "We advance to India in two days."

Kelly whistled a tuneless ditty and slowly inched farther and farther away from the group, trying to pretend she wasn't with these people and had never seen any of them before. When she tripped over the floor ashtray, sending it clanging to the floor, all eyes riveted on her.

Her room number was the first one called.

Bill looked back, hoping he had ditched the dark-haired stranger. He hadn't. The man was following—at a discreet distance, but still following.

Come on, you've been reading too many spy novels. You're letting your imagination run wild. He's probably going to the same hotel, that's all. Bill kept telling himself that, but the tingling nerve ends in the back of his neck contradicted the pat explanation.

Once inside the hotel, he joined the cluster at the check-in counter and tried to ignore the man leaning against the wall of the lobby, his black eyes staring at Bill without deviation. Now there was no doubt left in his mind that he was being followed.

His grip tightened on the briefcase and he felt once more for his passport. Could the man have seen all the equipment when he opened his briefcase earlier? Maybe he wanted the electronics. Admittedly he was now grasping for any explanation, but it was imperative that he know what the guy was after.

Bill cringed when the guide shouted out his room number and tossed him the key. That was the last thing he wanted the stranger to know. He turned around, wary, expecting the worst.

The worst happened.

The man barely shifted the lapel of his brown leather jacket to the side, purposely exposing the small black revolver that hung ominously in its shoulder holster.

Bill's eyes narrowed on the stranger's face, probing for explanations. Gone were the possibilities of a harmless pickpocket or desperate emigrant wanting a passport. This man meant business. But what?

Who the hell was this guy?

He took a deep breath to calm his racing pulse. One thing was certain. Whatever he wanted, Bill wasn't about to wait around like a sitting duck to find out.

After he had changed his own dollars for Deutsche Marks, he flowed with the group toward the bank of elevators. A thin line of sweat formed beneath the collar of his shirt as he watched the first elevator fill up before he could reach it.

The man was only a few feet behind him. He had to act fast. This was where he would outmaneuver the guy. He would go back into the airport on the ruse of getting a newspaper. If the man followed him again, he'd know this was no figment of his imagination.

As he pivoted sharply, his briefcase slammed into Damien Brewster's stomach. It registered in Bill's mind as nothing more than a slow start, so he didn't stop to acknowledge it. Instead, he shoved through the crowd, breezing past a surprised Jake Balletoni, and walked through the lobby, out the front doors, and across the covered walkway that led into the airport.

He stopped at the magazine counter and bought the *Herald Tribune*. When he turned around, he saw the stranger heading his way. Well, damn it! That's it. He was sick of this. He was going to find out what the guy wanted once and for all. He wasn't going to just keep running from him.

He hesitated for only a second, then started walking toward the man. But the dark-eyed stranger hesitated also, and when he moved again it was to reach for the revolver inside his jacket.

It registered in Bill's mind that this was more than a little misunderstanding, more than an insignificant mistake of some kind.

Whatever this person wanted was important enough to use a gun to get it, and Bill knew now that talking this thing out was not going to work.

Swerving to the left, he dashed across the large lobby. This was where his years of athletic training would not fail him.

He knew the man was behind him and, just as any true competitor knows where his opponent is at all times, Bill knew exactly how far behind. He was fast, but Bill was faster. And he would lose him.

He ran down the escalator and through the waiting room. He wasn't really sure where he was going, but he hoped to make it down to the connecting train terminal below. He turned to the left, keeping his peripheral vision open for the stairs. Swerving around passengers with luggage and traversing plastic chairs and information counters, he never slowed his pace. He ducked into a deli and exited through a side door. Finding the stairs, he descended. But there was no train station. He had made a wrong turn.

He leaned back against the wall, trying to catch his breath. Maybe he had lost the man. Maybe.

He waited. Waited for a dark-haired man he'd never seen before in his life to slip up beside him and press a revolver to his side.

The thought jolted him into action once again. But which way was he supposed to go now? Making a split-second decision, he turned left, following the wall until another stairway led back up to the terminal. As he rounded the corner, he was stopped short by a sharp jab in his stomach.

Gasping for air, he stared directly into the faces of two soldiers from the West German army, which policed the airport. Their rifles were held in front of them, facing the ceiling, and he realized then that it was the butt of the handle that he had run into.

"Haben Sie ein Problem, mein Herr?"

"I don't speak German," Bill groaned, holding his hand against his stomach.

"American?"

"Yes."

"Come."

Flanked by the two soldiers, Bill walked with them to a small office at the other end of the large terminal waiting room, dreading what was about to happen but, at the same time, aware of a cocky and self-confident relief at losing the dark-haired stranger.

Fifteen minutes later, a fat, loose-jowled officer named Reinhardt leaned back in his chair behind the desk and slapped Bill's passport between his hands. The briefcase sat open in front of him.

"So now, Mr. Clayton. Why were you running through our airport?"

"I was auditioning to replace O. J. Simpson in the Hertz ad."

The officer's expression was blank. "Why were you running, Mr. Clayton?"

Bill sighed. "What would you say if I told you that a man I've never seen, and with a reason I cannot imagine, has been following me with a gun?"

Reinhardt scowled at Bill for a good five seconds. "I would tell you to try again."

"That's what I figured." Bill, too, leaned back in his chair and stared at the officer, thinking. His mouth twisted cynically. "Okay, okay. A large wookie was chasing me because I have stolen the plans for the rebel alliance and I'm trying to make it to my galactic star cruiser." *What the hell, the guy may not know O.J., but everybody knows* Star Wars.

The officer glanced sharply at his subordinates and nodded his head. He leaned forward and folded his arms across the desk. "Good, Mr. Clayton, we are finally getting somewhere. Now suppose you tell me about this rebel alliance."

Kelly tried the calculations one more time. Now then, one Deutsche Mark is the equivalent of two American dollars. No, that's not

right. Let's see. Four dollars equals six
... no eight ... no ... She tossed the money
into the air and watched it scatter across the
bed. Okay, she flunked algebra, so what! She'd
try to calculate all this foreign currency business later. She picked up the bills from the
bed and shoved them hodgepodge into her
wallet.

She heaved her suitcase onto the mattress
and flipped it open, staring at the contents
and trying to decide what to hang up and
what to leave folded. There wasn't much
point unpacking all of it since they would be
here for only two nights. But she did pull out
a couple of dinner dresses and hang them in
the tiny closet.

After setting the suitcase on the floor in the
corner, she propped up a couple of pillows
and leaned back against the headboard. Roll-
ing up her pant leg, she checked the painful
bump rising higher by the minute on her
knee.

What was the matter with that guy anyway? Shoves his way through the crowd,
slams his briefcase into her knee and into
about three other people too. And doesn't
even stop to apologize! What could possibly
have been that urgent?

She touched her knee very lightly and felt
a burning sensation slide through her but

knew that it had nothing to do with pain. It was the thought of that briefcase, his briefcase, held in the grip of his hand. Earlier, in customs, his hand had reached across her thighs, the handle of his case gripped tightly in his fingers. She could still feel his other hand lying under her arm, his elbow pressed into the hollow between her breasts.

Funny, it had all happened so quickly after Damien Brewster knocked her off her feet. How was it that she could now remember every detail, every pressure point where his arm and hand had touched her?

You're getting carried away, Kelly. Has to be the jet lag. Nothing else could explain this attack of insanity. She stood up, and with officious zeal grabbed her notebook and pen out of her purse. She didn't want to think about him. First of all, the man was rude and arrogant. She would simply not think about him. She had too much else to do.

Maybe this afternoon she would go with the group into Frankfurt to visit the museums on the south bank of the Main or perhaps walk along the Zeil to do a little shopping.

On the other hand, maybe she would just stick around here and start working on her article. She needed to sketch a profile of everyone on the tour and jot down some general impressions of the trip so far. Though she wasn't happy about being here, she did take her job seriously. And even if the vacation was strictly for the budget-minded, the article had to be first class. But whose profile would she write first?

There was Damien Brewster, with his overwhelming Hai Karate cologne and open-to-the-navel shirts. There were the little old Caldwells who were too sweet to be interesting. There was Mrs. Willard, in white gloves and a pillbox hat overseeing the welfare of her precocious niece. And there was the sixty-year-old Winfred Rotterborg, who dressed like he was ready to scale the face of the Matterhorn. But the only sport Kelly had seen him involved in so far was that of wooing every female on the trip.

As quickly as each person came to mind, another image drove it away. Sandy-brown hair. Dark blue eyes that looked at her as if he had already seduced her and knew every taste and scent and texture of her body.

He was such an enigma. His physique was that of an athlete and yet he was an accountant. His eyes brought to her mind images of seduction, yet they remained securely closed to the man's own soul.

She tried to imagine what kind of profile she would write about him, but it was impossible. She remembered again the moment when he'd held her. *God, Kelly, are you insane! Get hold of yourself and stop thinking about that man. He obviously doesn't give a damn about you and you certainly shouldn't care about him. He is exactly the type of man you must avoid. Must, must!*

Bill walked into the hotel lobby and stepped up to the front desk. It had taken the better part of an hour to straighten out the misunderstanding with the military police. It seemed that his little *Star Wars* joke about the rebel alliance had not been well received.

Now all he wanted to do was retrieve his suitcase from the lobby, change rooms so that the man would not know where he was, and then relax for a little while. He thought of the bizarre turn of events that had taken place this past hour and puzzled over a plausible explanation for them. He could find none.

"I'm Bill Clayton," he said to the desk clerk. "I'm with Master Tours and I'd like to change my room, please."

The clerk checked his register. "Is something wrong with your room, sir?"

"No, it's just that . . ." Bill was thinking up a logical reason for the switch, but his gaze inadvertently swung to the far side of the lobby. Standing beside the escalator that led down to the bar was the dark-haired man. He

66

was looking the other way, but Bill knew that it would be only seconds before he turned back this way.

The desk clerk glanced at the clock to see how much longer he had until his lunch break. "Sir? Was there something . . ."

"No, thanks." Bill pushed away from the desk and walked briskly around the corner. There was another crowd of tourists waiting to file onto each elevator, but he knew he didn't have time to wait. He hadn't done it! God damn it! He hadn't lost him at all!

When the metal doors opened, Bill shoved past a couple of people and forced his way on. He was faced with an elevator full of disapproving frowns, but at least he was on. Right now that was all that mattered. And there was no room for even one more person.

Just before the doors closed, a large hand slipped in the slim opening, causing them to jerk back open, and Bill found himself face-to-face with the coldest pair of black eyes he had ever seen.

Jake Balletoni's expression never changed as he crushed his cigar in his hand and stepped backward, letting the elevator doors slide shut.

They opened on the sixth floor and Bill was the only one to get off. His thoughts were clustered haphazardly around one thing—the man who was still following him. He thought of the gun, the elevators, the rooms, the long hall, the door at the opposite end of the hall. The door. If the man wanted to be up here badly enough, he wouldn't wait for another elevator. He'd take the stairs. If he wanted to be up here! What a joke! He wanted Bill. Who the hell knew why. He just did.

Bill pulled his key from his pocket. Six twelve. He looked at the door numbers he passed. Six twenty-five, six twenty-three. Where the hell was six-one-two?

A hotel maid emerged from one of the rooms and pushed her supply cart back into the hallway. Bill's gaze jumped to the stairwell door. He looked at the room number on the door next to him. Six twenty. He looked back at the maid. She stepped into the hallway and threw something into the laundry cart. He heard a creak and his eyes moved to the stairwell. The heavy metal door began to open slowly, deliberately.

His lead time was running out. He could hesitate no longer. Without another thought he rushed toward the maid and placed his hand against the door only a second before she closed it. *"Danke schön,"* he whispered, stepping into the room and closing the door quietly behind him.

* * *

Kelly stepped out of the shower and rubbed her hair dry with a towel. She ran her fingers through the long strands to remove any tangles, dusted her body with powder, then wrapped the towel around her torso, tucking the ends in between her breasts.

She looked in the mirror to see if the shower had restored her looks as well as it had her spirits. The circles under her eyes were almost gone and her skin didn't have quite the sallow look it had after the long night on the plane. *Don't kid yourself, Kelly. You're twenty-nine and you look it.* So what? She wasn't trying to impress anyone. Of course, she did look a little better with her makeup on, but she would do that just before she left for the downtown tour this afternoon.

For now, she was going to take a short nap and relax. She had turned down the bed before her shower and the thought of cool sheets beckoned her into the other room. She walked halfway to the bed before it struck her that she was not alone.

She stared at her robe on the bed, but she knew, even in her state of fear, that it was ridiculous to think the man staring at her hadn't noticed she was in nothing but a towel. Her hand lifted to her throat in a paralyzing gesture of inadequacy.

Bill Clayton was standing in the middle of

her room, panting, sweat dripping off his brow. The look in his eyes reminded her of a cornered puma, poised, wary, and ready to strike with a huge, deadly paw if his opponent showed even the slightest signs of aggression.

Kelly didn't budge an inch.

CHAPTER FIVE

Kelly started to scream, but before she could emit the sound Bill dropped his stare and turned back to the door, ignoring her completely. It left her with a particularly unsettled, dissatisfied feeling. But she didn't reach for her clothes or run into the bathroom. The thoughts simply didn't occur to her.

Bill opened the door slowly, just a crack, in order to see down the hallway.

Appalled that she was standing there bewildered while a strange man took possession of her room and doorway, Kelly tried another tactic. "You have five seconds to get out of here before I scream bloody murder." There, that should get him.

The response was more silence.

"Believe me," she sputtered, "once I start, they'll hear me all the way to Munich."

Bill didn't turn around, but only waved his hand back at her with an impatient command to keep her mouth shut. Indignance pushed her chin up and out.

He watched through the crack in the doorway as the dark-haired man slipped stealthily down the hallway until he stopped in front of a doorway farther down.

Bill checked the number of the door across from where he was now standing. Six eighteen. His room number was six twelve. Counting the doors down to the one the stranger stood before, he landed on number six twelve. His room. The man was standing at his room!

He slipped a slim, knifelike tool into the keyhole, and the door opened. Bill watched as he pulled the gun from the shoulder harness and, pushing the door wide open with his free hand, entered the room.

Bill closed Kelly's door and leaned his back against it, frowning. What in hell was going on! He wiped his sleeve across his brow and took real notice of Kelly for the first time since entering the room. She stood there watching him, her face stiff with wary indignance, and it took several seconds for him to

72

process the fact that she was backing up to the telephone on the nightstand.

He was across the room the moment the receiver was lifted.

"No!" He yanked the phone from her hand and slammed it back onto its cradle. She started to scream, but before the meekest sound escaped, he clamped his hand roughly over her mouth. "No!" He wrapped one arm around her body, pinning both of her arms to her sides.

It was the scent of bath powder that registered first, catapulting through him with an acute awareness of the woman in his arms. He glanced down at the slim space between them and took note of the thin damp towel that separated her body from him. His eyes went back to her irate glare.

She struggled, but he tightened his grip. "Listen to me!" Assuming that she would obey him, he loosened the hold over her mouth. "I need your . . . Damn!"

Bill yanked his hand back and stared at the white indentations where her teeth sunk into his flesh. He stared at her, incredulous that she hadn't obeyed him.

In one swift movement he shoved her roughly to the bed, then fell on top of her. His hand was clamped tightly over her mouth again, and he held her arms immobile. "I'm not going to hurt . . . damn it, hold still!" His knee pushed between her bare thighs. "I'm not going to hurt you. But you have to listen to me."

The wrath in her eyes had turned to absolute fear when she first felt his body over her and his leg so possessively entwined with hers. What was he going to do to her? What type of man was he?

She wasn't stupid enough to think she could physically outmaneuver him. But surely there was something she could do to fight this.

He said he wouldn't hurt her if she would only listen to him. Well, all right, she would listen to whatever he had to say and then maybe, just maybe, he would go away.

She stared into his blue eyes, even darker and more unpredictable than she had remembered from this morning. A drop of sweat clung to his temple and she had the sudden irrational urge to capture it with her tongue.

"Someone is following me," he said. "He has a gun. He's in my room right now." His words were staccato, matching the strange, erratic beat in her pulse. She knew he was watching her eyes, waiting for her response, looking for any signs of disbelief. He must have seen some.

His jaw tightened ominously and the arm

around her felt even more constricting. "You have to believe me!"

"I do," she said, but no sound came out.

He stared at her mouth, watching the curve of her lips as they formed the words. He became aware of the rise and fall of her chest under him, the way their bodies conformed at certain angles. The pattern of his breathing altered substantially.

His jaw loosened, letting go of some of the anger, but his eyes never left her mouth. She felt the pressure of his knee between her legs increase almost imperceptibly and her breathing ceased as his face lowered to hers.

She knew he was going to kiss her. She could almost feel it already . . . the warmth of his lips against her own. She waited breathlessly for the moment to come and at some deep subconscious level was disappointed when it did not.

Bill was bewildered by the unreality of the moment. He was involved in some kind of game that had gotten away from him, a game for which he had been given no rules. A man with a gun chasing him. A beautiful woman lying beneath him.

His gaze slid down her cheeks and neck and chest to the knot in the towel between her breasts. It had slipped and was about to fall open. He stared at it, fascinated by the fragility and urgency of the moment.

Suddenly, disgusted with himself, he leaped from the bed and crossed the room. He opened the door and stared down the hallway again.

Kelly sat up on the bed slowly, secured the knot in the towel, and crossed her arms in front of her. She glanced at the black telephone on the bedside table, and thought once again about calling for help. She didn't. Her body was one trembling mass of nerves as she looked back at Bill peering out the slim shaft of her door. There was a bone-weary slope to his shoulders, and a puzzled anger in the hand that grasped the edge of the door so tightly.

She wished there were something she could do. Anything! Scream for help, hold him in her arms, throw something at him. Something! But there was nothing to do but sit in silence and watch him.

After a few minutes, Bill saw the door to his room open. In a kind of macabre fascination he watched the dark-haired stranger leave, walk down the hallway to the stairwell door, and disappear behind it.

He was gone.

Dazed, he turned around to look at Kelly, now sitting on the edge of the bed with a hand on the knot of the towel. There was a long expanse of leg exposed where the short towel stopped. White thighs that showed the beginnings of a summer tan.

He walked over to the bed, gently grasped her upper arms, and pulled her to her feet. There was a trembling of flesh beneath his hands and he sensed his hold on her was the only thing that kept her legs from crumbling beneath her. Her eyes were undeviating in their search for some answer that he didn't have, for a truth he couldn't speak.

His attention shifted to her fists clenched at her sides, the knuckles white, and he felt washed with self-loathing for the way he had frightened her.

"I'm really sorry . . . Kelly. I never meant to frighten you like that. I'm not that type of . . ."

Her breath caught in her throat as she waited for him to continue. He didn't. A drop of water slid from her hair down her temple and cheek. He wiped it away. His hand reached into her hair and his fingers wove through the damp tresses, lifting them off her shoulders. She felt the fingers wrap tightly around a wet strand.

His voice was drawn, pulled from somewhere deep inside him. "You don't understand what has been happening to me."

To you! she thought. *What about me!* Kelly

was scared. Scared of this man and whatever had driven him to barge into her room. And of her incredible reaction to him. Desperate to break the spell he'd cast upon her, she stared pointedly at his hand on her arm. "Are you through with me?"

He started to speak, but the words didn't come. He let go of her arm, and she felt every strand of hair sift through his fingers as he stepped back and stuck his hands into the pockets of his trousers. He walked silently to the door, peered out cautiously once more, then stepped into the hallway, closing the door quietly behind him.

Calmly, deliberately, she crossed the room, flipped the deadbolt, and inserted the chain lock. She pressed her forehead against the doorframe and did not move. She couldn't. All abilities, thoughts, and emotions were engulfed by the violent tremor that now rattled in the depths of her body.

The glowing red light on the telephone beside the bed drew Bill's attention and demanded that he do something about it. But he turned away, too tired to make the effort right now.

It was being so helpless that he couldn't abide. He knew that was what had exacted such a tremendous toll from him tonight. That was what it had to be.

He expelled a tight breath and walked to the window of his hotel room, looking out on the busy autobahn below. He stared at the bleak landscape but, in his mind, he was seeing another view, his old neighbor's house only six feet away, its chipped green siding partially eaten away by termites and disrepair.

Behind him his parents were having one of their nightly rows. The subject matter was always the same, only the tone was becoming more bitter, more wearisome.

"Why didn't you sign on down at the dock like Willie Soames's husband?" Winna Clayton's voice couldn't hide the fury that raged inside her as she stared down at her worthless husband.

William Clayton sunk lower in his chair. "I told you before, my back can't take it. You want me to end up a cripple?"

"Wouldn't be no worse off than you are now," she mumbled, turning back to the stove and throwing something green into the pot of stew.

"I didn't make the owners close up the plant, Winna. Goddamn 'em. Those bastards think they can run everybody's lives." He glanced over to the young boy at the window and his voice dropped lower. "And you know damn well why I don't have the schooling it takes to get a good job. It's not my fault."

Winna turned a bitter face toward him. "Nah, it's never your fault, is it?"

Bill smashed his fist against the wall beside the window, staring out across the smoky gray skyscape of Frankfurt. Well, he had never let it happen to him and, by God, he never would. The sins of the father would never be visited upon this son's head. He had made sure of that.

He had diligently studied his way through school, receiving a scholarship to Wharton where he graduated with an MBA. He had been a star pole vaulter and sprinter in college and had still maintained his position on the dean's list each semester. And he had moved up to a vice-presidency with his company in record time. No one would ever have control over his life. There was a solution to every problem, and he would be the one to find it, to have control.

What had happened to that control today? A stranger had followed him with a gun and he couldn't for the life of him figure out why. He wasn't ashamed to admit it; the man scared the hell out of him. If only he knew what he was after, he could deal with it, find the solution to it, bring it all under control.

He wiped the back of his hand across his mouth and a soft feminine fragrance wafted into his senses. He lifted his hand to his nose again and smelled. Bath powder. Kelly Milburn's.

In his mind he retraced the shape of her face so near his own, recalled the soft clean scent of her skin. He had held her beneath him with his knee between her thighs, pressing against her. He remembered how she'd shifted, only slightly, under him and a thousand needles of pleasure shot through him again.

Her eyes. She had the most beautiful, naked gray eyes he'd ever seen. An image of them filled with fear flashed before him.

His physical response to her was understandable. It was the emotional one he couldn't explain. A susceptibility of sorts, no doubt.

There was no room in his life for any weaknesses. And that's what this woman could become. He forced away the memory of his vows to change, to try to build a real relationship. There wasn't time for that now, with her. He would be around her for only two weeks. He could manage that—maybe even enjoy a few romantic evenings before the trip was over.

A sliver of doubt wormed its way into his

thoughts. Something told him it was not going to be as easy as all that to touch her and then just walk away.

He closed his eyes as the feel of her body beneath him came back to him, and involuntarily he lifted his palm to his nose once again, letting her scent shoot through him like a fireball.

CHAPTER SIX

Eunice Caldwell took the packages from Kelly's arms. "Thank you, my dear. Oh, but we made some wonderful buys in that little shop, didn't we, Henry?"

The elderly man frowned good-naturedly. "Don't know why we can't just sight-see like everybody else does. Can't figure out why we have to buy all this junk!"

Eunice clucked at Henry's grumbling and Kelly looked on with a skeptical smile, thinking the relationship between the two old people was just too good to be true. It was all so different from the conversations that had gone on in her own household. There had never been any wrangling or love-induced bantering between her parents. She couldn't recall much of anything between them, only a void, a silent chasm of boredom and despair and incredible loneliness.

"You are such a dear, Kelly darling." Eunice patted her arm while the rest of the group clustered around Mr. Angelique in the middle of one of Heidelburg's cobblestone pedestrian walkways. "What kind of article did you say you were working on?" Eunice asked.

"Travel story," said Kelly.

"I just admire you journalists so. Such inquisitive, investigative minds."

Kelly glanced away in embarrassment. "Oh, I don't know about that."

Eunice shook a gentle remonstrative finger at her. "Don't you deny it now. I know you never miss a thing."

Henry tugged Eunice's arm. "Come on, Mama. You're embarrassing the poor girl."

"Well, all right," she submitted, but as Kelly walked away, Eunice turned to Henry and the two of them exchanged a cold, precautionary look.

Bill hated puzzles. He liked everything easily recognizable, neat and tidy. He wanted to know the answer to every riddle. But Kelly

Milburn was a mystery, and he hadn't yet found the clue to solve her.

He followed the sighting of her camera, now directed toward an empty park bench. She had taken a whole roll of film today in Heidelberg. She had captured the three widows marching up and down the streets with their arms around each other. She had snapped the shutter as Professor Evanston tried to impress everyone with his knowledge of German history. She had caught each of their quirks and eccentricities with perfect timing.

But now, here she was standing in the middle of one of the oldest and most beautiful cities in Germany, taking a picture of an empty bench. Why? There were so many other things around them that were much more interesting. There was the ancient castle that had been built in the thirteenth century. It rose majestically high above the narrow lanes and picturesque maze of roofs. There was the Neckar River, or even the oldest university in Germany. But no, instead of that, Kelly Milburn was taking a picture of a bench with no one sitting on it.

He wanted to have her pegged perfectly. But something about her didn't fit the contours. Damn, he hated puzzles!

* * *

"Are you telling me we have to walk up to that castle, Angel!"

Lapito Ruta Migada Angelique sighed over Muffy's perpetual whine. If only her aunt would exert a little control over her, or muzzle her perhaps. He also wished she would say his name correctly, but had finally given up making his group call him by his real name and now he was simply Angel.

"Yes, Miss Muffy, we climb up."

Her disgusted huff could be heard across the circle of tourists and Kelly raised her camera to capture the gesture.

The guide walked over to her as she snapped her camera back into the case. "Hello, Miss Kelly."

She was still amazed at the bubble of excitement that was always present in the guide's voice. What on earth was he so cheery about! "Hi, Angel."

He started to correct her on his name, but decided that there were things in this world that one obviously could not fight. "How is your story? You have much material?"

"Some. It's coming along pretty well. You're not worried about it, are you, Angel?" she teased.

"Oh, my, my, my, my, my, my . . ."

Kelly laughed at the obscurity of the remark. "Was that a yes or a no?"

"No, no. I am not worried about the story. I know you will have wonderful time on this trip. You will want to tell the whole world."

"Yes, I'm sure," she smiled blandly. "But all I want to tell the world right now is how much my feet hurt. They are killing me. I think I'll find a pub, have a beer, and wait for the rest of you to come back."

"Ah, of course. Whatever you wish, Miss Kelly. We go now." He gathered in his flock and led them off, strutting in a column toward the castle.

Relieved that she was not joining the parade, Kelly detached herself from the tour and looked for the nearest bar. The one she found was filled with summer semester students from the nearby university. It was dark and smelled of wood and sausage and she found a table by the window where she could watch the local citizens pass up and down the walkway.

After she ordered a beer and a bratwurst, she slipped off her shoes, set her camera on the table, and sat back, relaxing for the first time all day. She had had enough of everyone's chatter and Angel's tour-guide spiel and just wanted a little peace and quiet to think.

Through the window she saw Mrs. Willard slumped over on a bench, sleeping away the tour to the historic castle. So far the woman

87

had not taken part in a single tour. It was a mystery why she even came on this trip in the first place.

Kelly's attention shifted to the young college couples in the pub. They seemed so carefree and happy, their hands and lips meeting in easy caresses, interspersed with cheerful laughter.

She wondered what it would be like to be that free and easy, to have experienced a time in life when everything was carefree. For her it had never been easy. And she couldn't think of a time she'd been carefree.

She tried to look away from the couples, but her eyes were drawn back to them time and time again as their mouths and fingers met. It brought on a rush of sensations that she'd just as soon forget. A mouth that could have kissed her but didn't, legs that lay entwined with hers, holding her helpless and weak and full of desire beneath him.

Why hadn't she screamed when she first became aware of Bill Clayton in her room? Why hadn't she thrown something at him? She could have and she knew it. There had been numerous opportunities when she could have yelled for help or even locked herself in the bathroom. But she hadn't. And it was the question why? that had tormented her throughout the day yesterday and all last night. It was as if she had wanted him to touch her . . . No, she didn't believe that! She wouldn't!

As though her fanciful images had projected him into the reality of the moment, she looked up to see Bill Clayton standing before her table. And as if she had been expecting him all along, he sat down in the chair across from her.

"Hi."

She looked away self-consciously.

"I hope you don't mind if I join you."

She didn't answer, but this time she looked directly at him. His eyes were like polished blue stones, cold and closed. And yet she remembered how warm they had appeared yesterday.

She sat quietly at the table, trying to remain impervious to the man across from her, but she softened a bit when she caught the troubled hesitancy in his expression.

He leaned his arms on the table and took a deep breath. "Things were so crazy yesterday that I don't remember if I apologized."

Kelly felt the first crack in the wall that encased her very shaky emotions. "You did."

"Well, maybe I owe you another one."

"Accepted."

He nodded and sighed, wishing he knew what else to say to make it up to her. But he had not had much practice at saying he was sorry. It had never seemed important enough.

Kelly kept her mouth tight and her eyes directed at the table. She was afraid to look at him because she knew she would immediately forgive anything he had done. "I could report you, you know," she said.

He looked surprised. "To whom?"

"To Angel." She didn't miss the sniff of amusement. "To the hotel management. To the police."

"So why don't you?"

She glared at him.

He leaned closer, his weight resting on his elbows. "Why didn't you call for help when I was there? Or why didn't you hide in the bathroom?"

Her eyes closed briefly. Oh, God, he had thought of those things too!

She opened her eyes again and stared, fascinated by the warm hypnotic rhythm of his voice, unable to control the moist heat that traveled through her body as she looked at him. "I don't have to sit here and listen to this," she whispered.

"That's right," he nodded. "You don't."

Kelly shoved aside her half-eaten sausage and stood to leave. His hand on her arm stopped her progress toward the door.

"Where are you going?"

"Walking."

"You told Angel your feet hurt."

"They feel much better, thank you," she replied in clipped tones.

"I think you're afraid to talk to me."

She stared at him, incredulous, not even realizing yet that he had dropped his hand from her arm and now leaned back in the chair with a half smile on his lips.

"You flatter yourself a little too much," she snapped. "Why should I be afraid of you?"

"Beats me." He smiled.

"I'm not afraid of anyone," she argued, aware of a constricting pain that traveled through her nerves with each lie. "Especially some man with a grossly overinflated image of himself."

"Don't go, Kelly." His voice was warm and low. "I think we need to talk."

She slowly eased down into her chair once again. "Okay," she sighed. "So talk."

He smiled, uncustomarily intrigued and delighted by her vulnerability. He leaned back in his chair and crossed his arms. "Have dinner with me tonight. I don't think I can handle any more group activities today. We could have a nice quiet dinner and then go back to your room." At her shocked expression, he added teasingly, "Your room is much nicer than mine."

"You are joking."

"No, my room is tiny. And your bed is softer than mine."

She couldn't believe the absurdity of this conversation. But her reply was almost as bad as his had been. "You weren't on the bed, you were on me."

They stared at each other for a long moment, Kelly wishing more than anything that she could take the remark back, he wishing more than anything that he could feel her against him once again.

His voice had lost the cocky tone and it came out in a low, soft rush. "You're right. Maybe it wasn't the bed that was so soft at all." He watched the blush travel up her neck and face and was suddenly sorry he had tormented her so. "Listen, I'm sorry." He laughed. "We've got to do something about this. I can't go through this whole trip apologizing to you all the time."

"Oh, I don't know why not," Kelly laughed, and looked across the room. The waitress, assuming she was signaling her, hurried over to her.

"I'm so sorry," the waitress said to Bill in broken English. "I didn't see you here. Would you care for a beer?"

"Yes, whatever you have on tap."

"And you, *Fräulein*? Would you like another?"

"No," Kelly said. "Just some water, please." When the waitress was gone, she turned her attention back to Bill. "Did you find out who was following you?"

He looked uncomfortable with the question. "Yes . . . sort of."

"Well?"

"Well what?"

"Who was he? What did he want?"

Bill hesitated, then shifted his gaze around the crowded bar. "It was nothing. Just . . . someone who wants something. I can handle it."

Kelly stared at him, saw the worried flicker in his eye, and knew it was more than nothing. She played with the paper napkin in front of her, debating whether to question him further.

Bill wasn't about to tell her about the message he'd received last night, or about the man named Jake. He didn't want to get her involved in this—whatever it was. He would deal with this in his own way, as he always had.

Kelly sighed, wishing he would tell her more, but resigning herself to the fact that right now he would not. She leaned back in her chair and crossed her arms. There was an awkward silence between them as they avoided any conversation by gazing about the pub as if it were the most interesting place in the world.

"So . . ." Bill leaned back and clasped his hands behind his head when he decided she had dropped the subject of Jake. "What's with all the empty benches?"

"I beg your pardon?" Kelly asked.

A large mug of beer was set before him. He took a long swig and set it back on the table before looking at her again. "You know, the pictures you take. Empty benches, lonely old women, dead trees, things like that."

She stared at him and clenched her hands repeatedly in her lap. "I don't know what you're talking about."

"Sure you do." He motioned to her camera on the table. "You take a lot of photographs of all the people on this tour . . . myself included, I would assume. But you also take a lot of really strange photographs that don't seem to make much sense."

She picked up her napkin from the table and began shredding it into tiny pieces. He watched her every move, wondering what it was that she was hiding. Wondering even more over the fact that he actually cared what she felt inside.

"I take pictures of things that interest me, that's all."

"What could possibly be interesting about an empty bench?" he asked, goading her on, knowing he was probably pushing too hard and too far, but unable to stop himself from doing it.

She picked up her water glass and took several sips, looking all about the bar, everywhere but at Bill. Finally she set her glass down and took a deep breath. She looked back at him. "You wouldn't understand."

"Probably not, but what the hell, why not give it a try?"

She sighed again. "It is a space in time I'm capturing, after the action has taken place." She watched his face for signs of comprehension. The immobile mask was in place. "You see, people sit on a bench. They talk with friends. Maybe lovers kiss for a while. Old men play checkers or reminisce. Business people read *Time* magazine or *Stern* or whatever it is over here in Germany."

She glanced away nervously. He wouldn't understand. He couldn't possibly. "You see," she said, looking back at him, "after the people have gone, after the interactions and the social contact and the emotions have gone, all that's left is the emptiness. After all of life's little moments, that's all that is left."

Bill stared at her for an eternally long minute, wishing he had never asked her, wishing she had never answered him, wishing he didn't know. She had exposed her weakness, her vulnerability, to him, and now he could never remain detached and impersonal. Damn, he wished he didn't know!

He set his empty glass on the table and stood to go, trying not to look at her. "I—I think I'll go try to catch up with the tour. Maybe there's still time to see the castle."

Kelly's hand was stuck to her glass of water and the other lay limply in her lap. She watched him go, sorry she had ever opened her mouth. It was just like in the photographs. The moment had passed. Again, all that was left was an incredible emptiness.

The weary tourists dragged themselves from the train terminal below the Frankfurt airport and ascended the escalator to the main terminal.

"Wait!" Angel cried. Still full of boundless energy and enthusiasm, he came tearing after his charges. "I forgot to tell you. Heidelberg is where they found a man five-hundred-thousand years old!"

The group was tired of hearing his tour trivia, so they continued moving onward without processing the information. Only

Winfred Rotterborg, still dressed in his Alpine mountain gear, responded. Turning on his heels, he planted both hands on his waist in rebuke.

"My good man, do you really expect us to believe that a five-hundred-thousand-year-old man was found living in Heidelberg?"

"Oh, my, no! He was dead," Angel reported.

Winfred started walking again, mumbling vague conjectures under his breath. "Well, I should hope so at that age." He looked back at Angel. "Now, don't try to pull those shenanigans with us, man. I tell you, we won't stand for it!"

"But . . . but, it was a study. An anthropo . . . po . . . po . . ." Angel watched his group walk ahead and he shrugged. Americans. He'd never understand them.

Bill let the others go on ahead of him while he walked to the locker he had rented in the airport late last night. He wasn't sure if Jake wanted what was in his briefcase or not, but he hadn't taken any chances. So, after he received the cryptic message, he had stored the case in a rented locker in the main terminal.

If it hadn't been for that message, he might have been able to denounce the whole escapade yesterday as a dream. But he had received it.

You have something I want and I won't stop until I have it. Jake.

Enigmatic and yet a clue. But what did he do now? As he stepped off the elevator on the sixth floor, the hallway was quiet and empty. There were no signs of the mysterious drama that had unfolded between these narrow walls yesterday. He carried his briefcase down the hall, slowing as he neared Kelly's room, and saw the door was ajar.

She was standing in the middle of her room, her face pale and wide with shock. All around her was chaos and devastation. He stepped into the room.

All of her things—her clothes, her notepaper, her books, her toiletries—everything was thrown about the room. Every drawer was pulled out and emptied, every cabinet and closet door thrown wide, and the bedcovers torn from the bed. Even her suitcase was emptied in the middle of the floor with its new blue lining torn to shreds.

"What the . . ." He moved to Kelly, touching her arm above the elbow. It was cold, as if an icy numbness had crept like a formless glacier up her body. "Kelly?"

She jerked her arm away and stepped back. It was several long moments before she spoke, her voice a frail whisper. "What has happened! What have you gottén me involved in!"

Bill stood motionless in the middle of the room while Kelly stared at him. "I don't know what you're talking about. This has nothing to do with me." He mouthed the words with a certain amount of belligerent conviction, but the doubt wavered in his eyes.

He turned away and stooped to pick up a pair of blue panties and a white blouse.

"Don't touch them!" she cried. "Don't touch anything!"

Bill laid the clothes neatly on the stripped bed, the bed on which only yesterday she had lain helpless and breathless beneath him. He pushed the thought aside and placed his hands on her shoulders. "Kelly, listen to me. You've got to look around and see if anything is missing."

"What?" She stared up at him, processing nothing that he said.

"You have to—" His words were choked off by a hungry flame that shot through his body, dividing him in two. He wanted to have no feelings for this woman, wanted not to care. He had tried all afternoon to push aside the images of emptiness she had described. He didn't want to know her that well. But something about her eyes now—the vulnerability, the anger, the involuntary desire as intense as his own—all expanded the other part of his thoughts until there was nothing left but an incredible thirst for her.

He watched the tears creep into her eyes and pulled her close, holding her head against his chest. Her hands clung to his shoulders, her fingers drawing the material of his shirt up into her tightly clenched fists as she cried.

"It's okay, Kelly. We'll get this worked out. Please, don't cry."

She pulled loose and backed away, running her hand through her hair. "I don't know where to begin."

Bill pulled himself into a tightly wound ball of self-discipline. "We have to call the management." He walked to the phone beside the bed and spoke distinctly, his dominant half taking over. "This is room . . . room six twenty. We need a manager and a maid up here immediately. This is an emergency." He replaced the receiver without waiting for any reply or questions.

He turned back to Kelly. "You have to look around and see if anything was taken."

She crossed her arms in front of her and looked about in frustration. "In this mess, how could anyone tell? Obviously whoever was here didn't break in for my underwear."

Bill tried to ignore the panic that was beginning to rise within her. He wanted to stick only to the pertinent facts. "Did you have any jewelry? Cameras? Did you leave your passport in here?"

She walked about the room, looking at everything, but being extremely careful not to touch anything. "There's nothing missing that I can tell."

"You're sure?"

"No, I'm not sure. I'm not sure of anything," she mumbled under her breath.

"Okay," he exhaled slowly, trying to remain calm and in control. "Now, it is possible . . . I mean, you might be right that this is not some isolated event or some second-rate burglary. Whoever came into this room was probably after something in particular."

Kelly's surprised gaze was on the verge of panic.

"Like what?"

"I don't know."

"You don't know or you're not saying?"

Bill was freed from answering when the hotel manager and a bellman entered the room and stared wide-eyed at the mess.

"What—what happened," the manager stuttered.

"I thought we asked for a maid," Kelly snapped. "Look at this place. I want it cleaned up. I want these clothes washed and . . ." The three men stared at her in awe as her body began to shudder violently. Only Bill had the sense to react.

He took her arm and pulled her toward the door. "Let them take care of this, Kelly. You've got to get out of here for a little while."

"But the room . . ." the manager sputtered. "There are questions to answer. The police must be contacted."

"Later," Bill said. "We won't leave the hotel. We'll be downstairs in the bar."

"But who did this!" the manager cried.

Bill cast a sharp glance at Kelly, wondering what her answer would be. But she only stared at him, through him, hiding her thoughts from his eyes. He breathed easier, realizing that at least for now she was going to guard his secret.

The sounds of easy jazz piano, clinking ice cubes, and low, seductive conversations filled the softly lit bar. But Kelly didn't hear any of it.

"What happened to the tour where nothing exciting ever happens?" she mumbled.

"What did you say?"

"Nothing." Her gaze passed absently about the bar. "Why do I feel like I've been invaded? I feel like the Norman conquerors

102

marched through my things." She stared into the drink Bill had ordered for her. "All of my clothes were touched by whoever did this." Her look was one of revulsion. "How can I possibly think about wearing them again!"

"It's not that bad, Kelly. You're overreacting because you're upset."

"Upset? Me? Surely you jest! Why on earth would I be upset!"

"They'll wash everything," he said.

"Tonight? We're leaving for Delhi in the morning, you know. This is a third-class tour we're on. I'll be lucky if they even give me another room to sleep in."

"You're welcome to come to mine, tiny as it is."

Her eyes narrowed suspiciously. "If I didn't know better, I'd think you staged this whole thing just to get me to your room."

"If I had thought it would work . . ." He shrugged and gave her what he hoped was a teasing grin. "You know, this might not have anything to do with what happened to me yesterday."

"I don't think you believe that."

His eyes locked with hers for a fleeting second, but his own face was a mask of reserve. Finally he shrugged. "I don't know."

"Well, aren't you even going to try to find out?"

"Of course I am."

"Then why won't you include me?"

Bill leaned his elbows on the table. "Kelly, I don't want you involved. I don't even want to be involved in this."

Kelly took a sip from her drink and wiped her finger along the condensation on the glass. Bill Clayton was such a handsome man, and very kind when he wanted to be. Was that the only reason she wanted to help him? She glanced up at his face and caught the worried frown. He was in some sort of trouble. He needed help, even if he wouldn't admit it to himself.

"I'm worried about you," she said softly. "I want to help."

He stared at her for a long, hard minute. She was worried about him! No one had ever been worried about him before. But Kelly Milburn, running her finger around the rim of her glass and staring down into her drink, wanted to help him.

"I can take care of myself, you know?" It was a feeble attempt to shut her out at best, and he knew it.

"I'm sure you can," she said. "But wouldn't it be nice to have someone help take care of you?"

Yes, he said to himself. *Yes, yes, yes!*

"Okay," he nodded after a long pause. "I'll tell you what little I know. His eyes lingered on the soft line of her mouth for a second before he began. "Yesterday when we landed, a man started following me. He was behind me all the way to the hotel. He had a gun. I had to get away from him. I did what I had to do."

His gaze swept across her face, then lowered to her breasts, now rising and falling rapidly. What he had to do. Yes, he had had no choice in the matter. Something stronger than his own self-preservation had called all the shots yesterday in her room. He'd had no control.

Kelly cleared her throat. "You don't have any idea why he was after you?"

Bill shook his head. "Not really. After I went to my own room yesterday, the message light was on. The message said that I had something he wanted and it was signed Jake. The only thing I can think of is the electronic equipment I'm carrying with me for my company."

"So why didn't he ransack your room looking for it instead of mine?"

He shrugged. "Maybe he did. I haven't been to my room yet." He glanced down at the briefcase beside his ankle, reassured that all was safe in his hands. "He wouldn't have found anything anyway. I hid my briefcase yesterday."

"But why would he search my room?" Kelly frowned. "Could he have seen you come into it yesterday?"

"He must have."

"But if he were looking for a briefcase full of equipment, why would he tear through my clothes and my makeup like that? It just doesn't make sense."

Bill was watching Kelly, impressed by the analytical approach she was taking to this. Maybe two heads were better than one. He had always solved his own problems without help from anyone, and he would solve this one too. But she did have a point. It didn't make sense. "I don't know," he answered. "Unless . . ."

"Unless what?"

He shook his head, then relented. "Unless he's not after the whole briefcase, but maybe just one thing in it."

"What are you carrying?"

"Just some circuit boards and computer chips for our doodlebuggers in Thailand." At her blank look he explained, "Geophysical crews. They search for oil."

"I thought doodlebuggers were water witches. What do they do, look for oil with willow sticks?"

Bill's smile was a bit patronizing. "Afraid it's a little more complex than that. There are a lot of different ways. They can drop explosive charges down holes in the ground, vibrate the earth's crust, or pop the ocean floor with air guns. The crew in Thailand is a vibrator crew. But the computer equipment I'm carrying is for the office in Bangkok. When the seismic data has been recorded on magnetic tape, it's processed on our computers so we can interpret. Kind of like drawing a map, only it's done on computers."

"Hmm," Kelly drawled, the beginnings of a smile easing away her tension. "All I know about computers are those games. You know, Pac-Man, Donkey Kong. I won the Ms. Pac-Man championship at our office."

Bill's expression drained to one of disbelief. "You have got to be kidding."

Her chin jutted out defensively. "No. Why should I be?"

He sniffed disdainfully. "I'm afraid this equipment is a little more sophisticated than that."

"Maybe you think so because you don't understand it. Sometimes things are simpler than people are willing to admit." Her body tightened imperceptibly as she realized how

107

much could be construed by her remark. She looked at Bill, but his mask was firmly in place, revealing no emotion whatsoever.

"So, what's going to happen to us now?" she asked, not at all prepared for the almost violent response from him.

"*Us?*" His eyes and mouth were wide open. "Nothing is going to happen to *us*. As of right now, you are out of the picture. I told you all of this because you wanted to know, but I'm not going to let you get involved."

"You can't tell me what to do, you know." She held her chin high, wishing she could get it through this man's thick skull that for some inexplicable reason she cared about him and wanted to help him. *But tread carefully, Kelly,* she reminded herself. *You're walking on the edge of fate with this man. You don't know what is going to happen with him when this is all over. Don't get too involved.*

Bill took Kelly's hand across the table. His thumb stroked along the back of her palm and he watched her fingers curl around his fingers. "Kelly, I . . . I like you. And I don't want you to get hurt any more than you have tonight." He felt dismal defeat and strange relief wash through him as he studied her. He had wanted to stay detached. But he had failed. It was the first time he had failed at anything in a long, long time. He wasn't sure he liked the feeling at all. "Please," he said, not sure what he was even asking for.

CHAPTER SEVEN

Fate or no fate, she could not get Bill Clayton out of her mind. Her thoughts of him were like a tightly woven ball of thread inside of her and she couldn't for the life of her find the end to untangle it. She had thought that when they left Germany, moved to a new environment, she could leave the knot of conflicting wants behind. She was wrong.

As if awakening from a warm, snug dream, she and the rest of the unsuspecting tourists were thrust into the harsh, dry reality of India. The smells, the sights, the voices, were unlike anything they had ever seen or heard before. This was not simply another country. It was another world. A completely alien way of life. But the feelings within her were the same. Everything had changed on the outside, but on the inside, nothing had changed.

When they landed at the Delhi airport, the group disembarked onto the tarmac and walked into the hot, dusty terminal. The hotel had indeed worked through the night to wash Kelly's clothes, and she bought several new outfits in a shop in the airport terminal. But now, her new pale blue short-sleeved blouse was sticking to her skin in the hot, oppressive air. And, already, her mind became obsessed with the one thing she couldn't have.

"God, if only I could have a tall glass of ice water," she sighed, closing her eyes to better see the mirage that lay like a cool, placid lake in her mind.

"Milk," someone else said. "I want a big carton of homogenized, pasteurized milk."

"I want a hamburger," Muffy complained, lugging her bag off the conveyor belt.

While waiting for their luggage, a young boy in a dirty gray robe offered Kelly a homemade cigarette. She wasn't sure what smelled worse, the Indian Beeri cigarette or the hot, spicy scent that rose from the pores of his small body. Declining the offer, she gazed around at the expressions of the culture-shocked people with whom she was traveling.

111

It was a look of panic that clearly cried, *Where the hell am I?*

As they passed through customs, Kelly took humorous note of the group members' various reactions. Leona Miller held a dainty lace handkerchief to her nose while Muffy adapted to the new environment by sharing the Beeri cigarette with the young Indian boy as a gesture of international goodwill.

Another form of global exchange was taking place only twenty feet away from Kelly, but with this one she could find nothing humorous.

Two men, identical in looks and dress had pulled Bill to the side. Their expressions were as intense and severe as their clothes, and Kelly puzzled over Bill's equally blank face. Considering what had happened already, these two men could only spell trouble.

"Bill Clayton?"

Bill turned to face the two men in twin blue suits standing before him with incisive, humorless expressions.

"Yes?"

"My name is Graves," the first man said. "This is Wilson. It is very important that we talk to you right away."

The skull-faced man named Graves pinpointed him with eyes that were little more than hollowed-out sockets, allowing no light to pass in or out of the cavernous gray orbs.

Bill's eyebrow rose a fraction. "And who may I ask are you?"

"We're civil servants, Mr. Clayton. Agents for the United States government."

"You have any identification?" Bill asked, baffled by what they would want with him but amused by their own self-assessment as servants.

Graves held open a small folder, Bill looked first at the left flap. It was the man's photograph. On the right flap was a card. He read the words CENTRAL INTELLIGENCE AGENCY, UNITED STATES OF AMERICA. It was followed by a series of numbers and the man's signature. Bill glanced at the other man and he, too, pulled out similar identification.

"We understand you are in possession of a certain computer microchip, given to you by two men in the Frankfurt airport."

Bill's expression tightened into one of caution. "What makes you think I have something like that?"

Graves sighed impatiently. "Our operatives in Frankfurt have been watching Kleinman and Dawson very closely. We know their every move."

"Kleinman and who?"

"Mr. Clayton, I think you do not understand the gravity of the situation at hand. The chip that Kleinman and Dawson gave to you was stolen from the United States government."

Bill's expression didn't change, but his thoughts were a shocked jumble of conflicting impressions. Stolen? The two men in Frankfurt worked with Lambert. It was a Lambert chip. How could it be stolen from the government?

Suddenly it struck him. This was all a joke! The guys back in the office in Denver had set him up for this whole charade. That was it. He started to laugh, but the two men before him were not laughing.

"We want the chip. It's really as simple as that. It belongs to the United States and the government wants it back."

The amusement died on Bill's face. "My information is that it was developed for geophysics data. For the Lambert office in Delhi."

"Let me ask you this, Mr. Clayton. The two men who gave you the chip, had you ever met them before?"

"No. But they said they were from Lambert. They had identification. They knew who I was. How would they have known that if they hadn't been with the company?"

"The other side makes it their business to know those things," Wilson said.

"The other side!" Bill laughed. "You must watch the same James Bond movies I do."

Again the two men did not laugh.

"Look"—Bill chuckled uneasily as he shook his head—"I'm an accountant. I work for a geophysical company. I'm not into all this spy business. Do you understand what I'm saying? I am an accountant."

The two men were either unconvinced or simply didn't give a damn what he did from nine to five. They were concerned only with the here and now. Whatever it was, Bill knew they weren't through with him yet.

Kelly edged closer to the men. There was something about them that she did not like at all. If only she could read their lips, know what they were saying. And why couldn't she understand the expression on Bill's face? It kept jumping from amusement to bewilderment to exasperation.

Maybe these were the men who destroyed her room. One of them might be Jake! A spark of anger threaded through her bloodstream as the idea of vengeance formed like a sluggish stream in her mind.

She was going to find out about this. She wasn't going to just sit back and allow danger to surround her when she didn't even know what was going on. After all, it had been her room that they ransacked, not Bill's. Why should he be privy to all the facts and juicy details when she had none? This was just all too exciting to ignore it. She wanted in!

Her decision made, Kelly strode purposefully up to the three somber men, ignoring the curious hostility that flowed outward from the two strangers.

Bill turned to find Kelly standing beside him, audacious curiosity adding a glimmer of light to her gray eyes. Sighing impatiently, he ceased his conversation with the men. He didn't need this. Noticing the hostile stares of the two agents, he knew it was imperative that he get her out of the picture immediately.

"See if they can hold the bus for me, Kelly. I'll be there shortly."

Her mouth tightened at his abrupt demand, but she forced down the humiliation and turned in search of Angel. She would take care of Bill Clayton later.

"We will take you to your hotel," Graves said. "The bus can go on."

Bill looked back at Kelly, who was still standing close by, listening for his reply.

His jaw snapped once before his answer was ground out between clenched teeth.

"Have Angel put my bag on the bus, Kelly. I'll be there in a minute."

Graves and Wilson exchanged sharp glances that carried a world of meaning only the two of them could interpret.

"Who is she?" Graves asked.

"None of your business," Bill answered crisply.

They both watched Kelly walk away, analyzing every detail about her before they continued. "Mr. Clayton, you are an intelligent man, so I think it only fair to explain to you exactly what the situation is that we're dealing with."

"I think that would be wise," Bill said, not fooled for a minute by their intelligent-man routine.

"Last week, Thursday, to be exact, an East German scientist named Hans Gretchel defected to the West. Dr. Gretchel was a member of a team that was working on a highly secret computer design for the next generation of Soviet spy satellites. You must realize that this young man's position is very sensitive and that he has information that could be highly useful to the United States."

"In other words, he's going to tell you how to design one of these chips."

"No, Mr. Clayton. He smuggled the chip out with him."

Bill's gaze shifted to the briefcase that he held so tightly in his grip. "And you're saying the chip I have belongs to this scientist?"

"No. It belongs to the United States government. Gretchel turned it over to our officials in West Berlin last week as payment for asylum. It was stolen on Saturday from the agent's hotel room."

"Guess that agent had better start looking for another job," Bill quipped, still refusing to take these two men as seriously as they took themselves. How could he even be sure they were really government agents? Jake must have been after this chip, too, and he was certainly no good guy. At that thought Bill began to get nervous . . . and angry.

"Mr. Clayton." Graves was becoming increasingly abrupt. "This circuit, in the wrong hands, could spell dire consequences for the entire world. The very security of your country is involved here. You have an obligation. . . ."

Fed up with their officious zeal and whole situation, Bill pointed an accusing finger at the man. "Listen to me! I am a businessman. I am trying to get along in this world the best way I know how. I don't give a damn about East-West subterfuge, intelligence networks, spies and double agents. Besides that, I don't trust you and I don't like you or the way you're trying to manipulate me."

The two men remained stoically erect and proper, the expression on neither one altering even a degree.

"Now, the chip was given to me by two men who claimed to be connected with my company. So I will keep it until someone from my office tells me that it does indeed belong to the United States government."

Assessing the situation and the man with whom they were dealing, Graves decided to take a different tactic. He pulled a piece of paper out of his pocket and, with a government issue pen, wrote a number on it. "This is the American embassy in Delhi. Call this number. You can confirm the information we have given you."

Bill took the slip of paper. "I'll call from the hotel."

"Mr. Clayton"—Wilson clamped an intimidating hand on Bill's arm—"please call from here . . . now."

"Mr. Bill, Mr. Bill!" Angel came running over to the three men, Kelly at his side. "You going to miss de bus, Mr. Bill. We must go. Now."

Bill felt the clutch of Angel's hand on his shirt and he gave one final taut smile to the government agents.

"Mr. Clayton, we are not finished talking with you," Graves sputtered. "You must make that phone call . . ."

Kelly planted herself before the two men, her fists perched in implied threat on her waist. "Listen here, you big—"

Bill grabbed her arm and began dragging her away from the men before she could complete her combative denunciation of their character.

"Vewwwy dangerous, Mr. Bill. Vewwwy dangerous." Angel clucked his tongue before darting off to gather up the rest of his scattered flock.

Bill looked back at the two men and frowned. Something wasn't right. Graves and Wilson were standing back there, looking like they were about to explode, but didn't know what to do about it. It didn't click. If they were CIA, why had he got away so easily? No, something was very wrong with this.

He looked down and realized he had hold of Kelly's arm. "What did you think you were doing over there?" he growled, worry over her safety making him sound harsher than he'd intended.

"I intend to find out who ransacked my room and why," she snapped.

His hand tightened its grip. "Well, you're going to get hurt. This is getting more com-

120

plicated and probably more dangerous than I realized. So I want you to stay out of it. Is that clear?"

"No, it is not clear. I told you before, if you are not interested in finding out what's going on, I am. Don't try to bully me."

Kelly stopped, wrenching her arm from his hand, and stood before him, halting his stride toward the bus. Eyes blazing and fists clenched, she was no longer aware of the pain that she was allowing to escape. "I have been bullied all my life. Don't you dare try to play my father with me, because I've had that kind of abuse up to here!" She sliced her hand across her throat for emphasis, then turned and stalked off toward the bus, leaving a stunned Bill watching her.

He followed her to the bus, unhurriedly, confused at the bitter tone in her voice. What had he done? What did she mean, trying to play her father? All he was trying to do was keep her from getting hurt. Didn't she understand that? He didn't want her help!

As she lifted a leg to climb onto the bus, exposing a brief glimpse of thigh beneath her unbleached muslin skirt, he was aware of a thread of desire that slipped into his pores and wound through his body, but he denied it vehemently. He did need her help. He wanted her with him. For despite his at-

121

tempts to remain free and clear, Kelly's own insistent imprint had seared its unmistakable brand into his heart.

Jake saw it all. Graves and Wilson with Bill Clayton. But what in hell was the security personnel of Randall-Impex's interest in this chip? Randall-Impex, like Lambert Technologies, was involved in everything from building aircraft to making video recorders for home viewers. Was Clayton going to sell the chip to them? They didn't look very happy with him and he didn't give them the ceramic case.

And what was the deal with that broad? Where did she fit into this scheme? He had cleaned her room out good the other night, looking for the chip. He didn't really expect to find it there. It was more as a warning gesture for Clayton. If he cared about the girl, he'd better give up the chip. Face it, Clayton, Jake laughed to himself. The game is almost over.

Bill glanced at the phone beside the bed and reached for the receiver. He looked down at the piece of paper in his hand, thinking about the two men in the airport. What in hell was going on? This was absolutely crazy!

"I really think you ought to call Fritz Graber."

Bill looked up at Kelly standing across the room, watching him with excited eyes, impatient for him to make the call.

"And don't look at me like that," she added with a laugh. "You're not going to get rid of me that easily. I'm a very persistent person. Besides . . ." She looked away and cleared her throat. "I'm worried about you."

He studied her closely for a minute, then looked again at the slip of paper with Fritz's phone number. He had already called the number the two CIA men had given him, and that had turned out to be a nonworking number. Now, as much as he hated to admit it, he knew Kelly was right. He had to call Fritz Graber.

Trying to pretend that it was his decision and not hers, Bill picked up the phone and slowly dialed the number Dawson and Kleinman had given him.

"Graber here." There had been only one ring before the voice answered at the other end.

"Hello, this is Bill Clayton."

"Ah, yes. I've been waiting for your call. Are you in your hotel?"

"Yes."

"Any problems?"

Bill's expression was solemn. The question could have been an innocent one, but for some reason he didn't think so. "There's a slight one."

Silence ensued at the other end of the line. "What kind of problem?"

Bill hesitated, uncertain about even Fritz Graber's role in all of this. "CIA," he finally said.

"What?"

"Central Intelligence Agency."

A long stretch of strained silence once again greeted him from across the wire. "And?"

Bill frowned at the man's lack of concern. "And you don't sound too surprised."

"Mr. Clayton, why don't you just tell me what transpired."

Bill was suspicious and becoming more so by the minute. At the same time, he had to get some information and right now Graber was the only source. "There were two of them. At the airport. They said the chip given to me in Frankfurt was stolen from the U.S. government. Supposedly a special design for Soviet spy satellites, smuggled out of East Germany."

"Did they now." Graber paused, collecting thoughts that Bill could not read or predict. "And the two men in Frankfurt who gave you

124

the chip—Kleinman and Dawson—what did they tell you?"

Bill's eyes narrowed in confusion. Why would he ask something like that? "They told me it was for my company. What the hell is going on here?"

Graber spoke slowly, methodically, as if he were gathering the facts into his brain only a second before he actually related them. "The chip was not developed for your company, Mr. Clayton. Lambert designed it for the U.S. Defense Department. It was to be used in one of the new test missiles."

"Then why was it given to me?"

"Because it was necessary to get it out of Germany in the quickest and most secure way possible. You were the likely choice."

"Well, that's just great," Bill grumbled, accepting the possibility for the first time that he had been used as a pawn in his own government's game of cat and mouse. "So what do I do about these two James Bond clones?"

"I don't think they were really CIA agents. They could be with the other side."

"Could you come up with a more original phrase?"

"You must be very careful," Graber continued after a short pause. "There will be a lot of people who will try to get the chip from you. Don't trust anyone. Anyone."

"Does that include you?"

Ignoring the question, Graber laid out precise instructions where and when Bill was to meet him. "This will all be over for you in a little while, Mr. Clayton."

"What is that?" Bill asked.

"Your inconvenience."

Inconvenience. Bill's face was grim. Only two days before he had assured Kleinman and Dawson it was no inconvenience. He glanced over at Kelly—she was leaning against the wall with her hands behind her. Now he knew better. "Good-bye."

Bill hung up the receiver and stared at the black phone for a minute, thinking.

"I want to meet this Fritz," Kelly said.

He let out a quick sigh and shook his head. "Kelly, Kelly, Kelly. I can't let you do that."

Her expression was determined, leaving little room for debate. "Why not?"

"Because, for one thing, you could get hurt."

"What else?"

He laughed in disbelief. "You need more?"

"You could get hurt, too, you know."

"I can take care of myself," he said.

"Well, so can I."

Bill shook his head in exasperation and walked over to her, towering over her shorter, slighter frame. "I don't get you." He smiled in bewildered amusement down at her. "Is this some sort of game to you? I am in possession of a computer chip that a lot of people want. I don't know why they want it. I don't know what it's for. I don't know anything anymore. All I know is that I have it and they want it. I'm not even sure how far they'll go to get it. This is not one of those video games you play, Kelly. This is real life."

Kelly stared up at him, refusing to be intimidated by his patronizing tone, but feeling, nonetheless, the ever-increasing tension of his body so close to her own.

"I know it's not a game, Bill."

"Do you?" His voice had dropped lower and she felt the heat from his eyes moving across the planes of her face and neck in a weakening caress.

Kelly's lips parted, but the words she wanted to say wouldn't come out. And yet they played loud and clear in her own mind. *For once in my life I'm doing something. I'm experiencing life, not just watching it pass by me.* "But there is a sense of . . . excitement, Bill."

The word echoed through both of their minds while the actual thrill of it rippled like currents of electricity between them. He reached out and touched the ends of her long brown hair bringing some strands up to his

127

face, feeling their texture against his cheek. His face moved closer; his body leaned in toward hers. There was an inexorable pull that closed the space between them, slowly, enticingly, drawing the power and vulnerability from each of them and combining it in a field of energy that was both impetuous and searching.

Excitement.

"Yes." The deep sound escaped the trapped confines of his throat as his mouth dropped down to hers, sampling the flavor that had been teasing his mind's palate for three days.

Their lips touched, then parted, then opened and touched again. He sampled her lower lip first and then moved to her upper lip. A force within him took control, tunneling into her mind and body and making it his own. Everything she had was suddenly taken from her. His mouth pulled the unguarded sweetness from her, his hands branded her flesh with their possessive heat, his heart pounding next to hers ripped her soul from her body, and his lower body pressed into her until she was helplessly trapped in the desire that had exploded between them. Her hands went to his shoulders to offer the possession he so badly needed. Both of his hands were now in her hair, his fingers moving through the long brown strands, and she was aware of a burning sensation where the tip of every finger touched her scalp.

Bill pulled his mouth away from the corners of her lips and stared down at her, his eyes reflecting the surprise and want that ravaged his mind and body at this moment.

When he spoke, his voice was low and quiet, the words torn from somewhere deep inside the man. "You kind of push me, Kelly. It scares me a little. You say you've been bullied all your life . . . well, I've been pushed too. All my life. I—I want you. And I even want you with me on this, but . . ." He closed his eyes briefly before opening them to beseech her. "Please, just don't push me."

Her hands dropped over his shoulders and slid slowly down his chest. Her own eyes were moist with the sensations she had been unable to deny or control. She didn't want to push him. She didn't even know what she wanted or needed anymore. Bill Clayton had mixed up everything for her. "Does this mean I can go with you to meet Fritz Graber?" she whispered.

She was his weakness. He knew that. He would accept it—for now. He was away from home and that made it easier. The breath he had been holding in was expelled in one short burst of conflicting emotions. "Yes, damn it, yes."

CHAPTER EIGHT

They rode the elevator down to the lobby of the Oberoi, taking in the view of the pool and patio from the large glass windows as they walked across the marble foyer. The blistering rays of the sun lay like a huge yellow blanket over the few bathers who had braved the heat. Beyond the wall that surrounded the pool and garden lay a thick grove of trees, and beyond that a few graystone buildings rising above the highest branches.

A taxi was waiting for them at the front of the hotel and Bill held the back door open for Kelly. It was a small Ambassador, as were most of the cars in India. To increase national production, the government discouraged the importation of all foreign automobiles. So, a cramped Ambassador it was.

"We want to go to the war memorial. Do you know it?" Bill spoke slowly and distinctly to the driver.

"Yes, yes, yes. Of course! I will take you there. I will take you anywhere. You want to see the capitol? You want to see the grave of Gandhi? You want to—"

"We want to go to the war memorial, that's all."

The driver shrugged, puzzled but not completely surprised by the American's lack of interest in his city.

Kelly leaned up against the back of the front seat and frowned at Bill. "We would love to see the rest of the city," she said, "but we're on a tour. And right now we have to meet someone at the memorial." She sat back and glanced sideways at Bill.

Bill scowled. Okay, so he had been rude. He was preoccupied, damn it! She was bubbling over with excitement about all of this. He was worried.

He held the tiny ceramic case in his hands, turning it over and over, his mind also turning over all the possibilities this small computer chip implied.

He looked up at Kelly and shook his head.

"I will be so glad to get rid of this . . . this albatross."

"Aren't you the least bit curious about what it is?"

He nodded slowly, not really wanting to admit that her feverish inquisitiveness was beginning to affect him. "It bothers me in a way. Basically, I keep worrying that maybe it's going to end up in the wrong hands."

"Then you think it is something for the government, something for missiles or spy satellites?"

"Well, it certainly isn't for Ms. Pac-Man." He stared at the tiny chip. "And I don't really think it's for geophysical data either."

"Then what?" she asked as Bill slipped back into his brooding silence without an answer.

Kelly's eyes followed the clean lines of his face and neck, aware of a solidity and strength in his character that filtered through the hard casing of cynicism. She wanted to touch him, had the need to know certain things about him, but she didn't dare move her hands from her lap.

She turned her attention instead to the passing scenery, catching it all as a blur of rose and burgundy bougainvillaea, bright splashes of color along clean, wide boulevards.

Where was the India she had always heard and read about? The one where people lived on top of each other in festering squalor? It certainly didn't exist here in New Delhi. Here the British influence still reigned in the architecture and the flower-draped avenues that led to the center of the city.

And yet there was something unreal about it. Some intangible quality that made you suspect instinctively that all of this was a façade, that the earth-colored buildings and British gentility were window dressing that hid from view the stark, realistic elements beneath.

Only hints of its existence reared their heads every so often. Naked children sitting alongside the road making patties for sun-dried bricks out of oxen or cow dung, fathers pedaling bicycles and towing their families behind them in two-wheeled carts.

It was there, but here along the gracious flower-bedecked avenues of old Victorian homes, it was not visible.

Bill looked out his window, seeing nothing, thinking only of the woman sitting beside him. She was nothing like the other women he had known. Sure, she was beautiful and desirable, but he'd never had trouble finding women with those attributes. It was more. He knew it, but he tried to deny it. She had a vulnerability that tugged something within him. And what was worse was that he wanted to share it with her. He didn't want her to be alone.

He wondered if thoughts of Lisa would take his mind off Kelly. Maybe she was only a passing fancy the way Lisa had been. Lisa, yes, he would think about her. After all, she was beautiful, too, plus he had dated her off and on for almost a year. And talk about insecurities! He tried to focus his thoughts on her, tried to picture her perfectly in his mind, but the image was fuzzy around the edges. As chauvinistic as he knew it was, it was Lisa's legs that had first attracted him. But there wasn't much else about the ballerina that had made an imprint. Funny, he had seen her only a few days ago, but he couldn't seem to put the pieces of her face together into a coherent whole. She had been reduced in his mind now to nothing more than a great pair of legs.

He glanced at Kelly as she watched the blur of homes and cars and people outside the window. Her long hair was tied back in a ponytail and her gray eyes seemed to pull something from the scenery that no one else could see. It was the same when she looked at him; it was as if she suspected what was beneath the layers of toughened hide and wouldn't stop looking until she found the truth within him.

He swallowed the fear that lay down deep.

Maybe . . . He swallowed again. Maybe she wouldn't much like what she found when she got there.

The driver edged into the curb. "This is the war memorial."

Bill's head shot upward to the large, sand-colored stone archway in front of them, and he shoved all personal thoughts away. Fritz Graber would be here. He would take the chip off his hands. His concern with it would soon be over. "Thanks."

"You want me to wait?" the man asked.

"Yes. We'll only be a few minutes."

Kelly opened her door and stepped out onto the curb, and Bill followed.

The monument sat in the middle of the boulevard, flanked on each side by a park area. Men in baggy white pants and shirts, cloth wrappings on their heads, were milling around at the base of the large structure.

"Do you see him?" Kelly asked, squinting her eyes against the blinding sun. She rummaged around in her purse for several seconds, searching in vain for her sunglasses.

Bill squinted into the sun, causing tiny white lines to fan out from the corners of each eye. "He said he'd be wearing a blue jacket, but I don't see . . . Wait a minute. Is that . . . That could be him over there." There was a breathless quality in his voice, a deep-toned excitement, a crisp crackle of adrenaline in the staccato of words. "Let's go."

They started walking toward the monument. Bill's stride was quick, incisive, full of tense vigor and athletic zeal, and Kelly had to struggle to keep up. The other man—Fritz—was walking with an equally determined gait from the other side of the arch toward Bill and Kelly.

Each of their strides was orchestrated to a purposeful beat. A syncopation of steps that would surely bring this all under Bill's command. He would have the problem in hand. He could get on with what he came on this trip for. Relaxation.

They were only fifty yards apart and Bill raised his hand in greeting. Graber lifted his arm, but stopped the movement at mid-chest.

Something was wrong. Bill felt the pliability congeal in his bones. Something was terribly wrong.

Even from this distance he read the look of panic on Graber's face. The man's head swiveled, followed by the sharp pivot of his body. A green Mercedes, registering in Bill's mind as an abstract oddity among the multitude of tiny Ambassadors, crept along at a snail's pace behind Graber, moving closer, sliding into the curb beside him.

Graber bolted, his feet pounding the pavement as he dashed toward Bill. The car sped up, cutting off all distance acquired by Graber's heavy, lumbering jog.

He was too slow. The car was too fast.

The car skidded to a halt only forty feet in front of Bill and Kelly. The back door swung open. Two men jumped from the backseat. Automatically Bill threw his arm out, holding Kelly back. His heart was pounding. His breath was coming in ragged gasps, and he was only vaguely aware of her fingernails digging into his outstretched arm.

The two men grabbed each of Graber's arms and dragged him into the back of the Mercedes. With liberating energy the car shot away from the curb, its tires screeching against the hot, dry cement.

Bill turned to race after it, his feet thudding in perfect unison with his heart. Kelly followed, but her shorter legs were no match for his.

The car sped down the wide avenue, disappearing almost mystically in a haze of heat that rose in searing waves from the parched pavement. In less than a minute the car and Graber were gone.

Kelly stopped and gasped for breath, realizing she could no longer keep up with Bill. She closed her eyes and tried to slow her breathing to ease the pain in her chest where her heart was pumping so fast. Bill had stopped about twenty-five feet away and was standing at the edge of the street, his eyes riveted on the car as it retreated into the fog of heat.

Kelly cast a quick gaze around the area, trying to gauge the reactions of the bystanders. She saw none. Everyone simply wandered along on their own way, oblivious to the drama that had unfolded before their very eyes.

Her gaze landed on a taxi parked across the street. A dark-haired man was standing on the sidewalk, leaning his burly arms against the top of the car as he stared at Bill.

Her heart began a rapid, spasmodic thump and she felt a curious tightening along the skin at the back of her neck. That man. She knew that man from somewhere.

As if to fill in the missing pieces, he pulled a cigar from his shirt pocket, bit off one end, and jammed the other into his mouth.

That was it! The man from New York. He had been on the same flight the tour was on from the States. My God, he was following them!

"Bill!" Kelly shouted and began running toward him, cursing the impracticality of the strappy sandals she had worn. "Bill, that . . ." With a small cry Kelly caught the heel of her shoe in the loose dirt of the sidewalk and stumbled, falling down to the ground and landing on one knee.

She cried out again, then bit her lower lip in dismay over her stupidity. Bill squatted down beside her, the fine lines on his face creased with concern.

"Are you all right?" His hand touched her hair, and stroked her back. He started to help lift her, but she clutched his arm to stop him.

"Listen to me," she whispered. "That man . . . across the street. I've seen him before!" Ignoring her anxious ramblings, he tried once again to lift her up and this time succeeded in pulling her to her feet.

"Bill, look at him!" she cried. "Over there!"

Bill followed the line of her gaze to the car and she felt the erratic pounding of his heart so close to hers. His face was frighteningly composed, yet his eyes were washed with defeat.

He never let go of Kelly, but he watched Jake throw the unlit cigar to the sidewalk and climb into the backseat of the taxi. Wrapped in the illusive safety of each other's arms, they watched the taxi pull away from the curb and head in the direction opposite from the one the Mercedes had taken. The car passed under the archway and was lost in the web of the government buildings ahead.

Jake, Graber, CIA, Lambert. What in hell

was happening in his life? He was to meet Graber, but someone got to him first. They probably wanted the chip and therefore probably wanted Bill. That was it. They took the wrong man!

He looked down at Kelly. Still, out of all of this, she was the most bewildering new element in his life.

With sudden clarity Kelly became aware of her hand against the back of Bill's neck, the feel of his warm, moist skin beneath her fingers. Her other hand was on his chest and the thudding in his heart changed tempo, but never slowed. He was looking down at her, his arms wrapped around her waist. And where her blouse had pulled loose from the waistband of her skirt, his fingers dug into the soft flesh of her side.

Their faces were so close, and their breaths mingled in the throbbing energy of the moment.

As in the earliest days of man's survival, fear evoked fire and, in turn, that same fire aroused a fear of its own. A dread that once the flames were allowed to go unchecked, their heat might run rampant, out of control, as wild as the passion that incited it, overcame both Bill and Kelly.

A convulsive warmth traveled the length of her body as Kelly stared up at Bill's searching face. His eyes revealed the sensuous heat that was engulfing him and yet she could also feel his tension. He was worried. He was frustrated. And he was consumed by the labyrinthine maze that pulled them both further and further into its shadowy twists and turns.

As they stood together amidst the scattering flames that scorched and gnawed at their insides, they both knew one thing was certain. The matter that had brought them together had changed, and the rules had somehow evolved to a new level where all the players—even the two of them—were now playing for keeps.

This was no longer a game.

CHAPTER NINE

The song was always the same. It would come to Jake in the middle of the night sometimes, sad and sweet, and always tormenting.

It was a plaintive ballad of woe and loss, about a peasant family whose sheep have died, leaving them no source of income. The family's only hope lies in their eldest daughter, Rosa, who must leave home to find work in the city to support her brothers and sisters. But alone and friendless, Rosa dies from hunger and cold.

In the final stanza of the ballad, her father's tears douse the last embers of their dreams and hopes and, pulled by a gray, flea-bitten mule, Rosa's flower-draped body is carried home in a wagon.

It was not the song itself that affected Jake so much, for almost all the songs of Sicily were sad. It was the young balladeer he had loved. Rosa Dolci. Her long braids, like coarse brown wheat, had coiled loosely on each side of her head, the young, sweeping curves of her body lay unrestrained under her frayed peasant skirt and blouse.

Jake leaned back against the pillows on his bed and closed his eyes. Rosa.

The braids had come down for him.

But other visions also haunted his mind. Other women. The dark-eyed beauty he'd known in Damascus. Her long black hair swirling about her head as she danced, hips that gyrated, eyes that sparkled with wicked delight, legs that had lain entwined with his through many long nights. There were the American women, too, but they did not impress him much. Too skinny, too pushy, too smart.

Yet despite the collage of feminine faces that danced like naked nymphs in his inner vision, it was always the face of his first, sweet Rosa that lay like a soft down quilt against his heart, her sad songs reminding him of how far he had come and how much he had lost along the way.

144

Stubbing out his cigar in the ashtray beside the bed, Jake grumbled out loud. He hated sentimental reminiscence. Such a waste of valuable time.

It was all because of Clayton and that good-looking broad who had attached herself to him. He'd watched them this afternoon. He saw the looks, the touches. He was no fool. They were getting close, too close. She'd just better watch her step or she was going to be in as much trouble as her boyfriend was.

Several new developments had presented themselves today. The rendezvous at the war memorial had been most interesting. It had all happened too fast for him to see who the people were in the Mercedes. Could it have been Graves and Wilson again?

They had grabbed the man Clayton was supposed to meet, but Jake didn't recognize him either. He was obviously someone who'd made a deal with Dawson and Kleinman and was trying to carry it out with Bill Clayton.

New developments to ponder, all right. But hell, it was no problem. He'd figure it all out in the end. He always did. He pushed away the isolated thought that if he were younger, he would have had this all wrapped up by now. Age had a funny way of sneaking up on a man.

The big question now was how much this

Milburn girl knew about the chip, and how difficult she was going to make his job. If she got in the way, she'd have to expect the same treatment as Bill Clayton could expect. Nobody was going to get in his way.

Jake sat up on the bed and reached for the phone. He had already tried to reach George several times at his home in Dallas, but his wife didn't know where he was. This time he dialed directly to Lambert's headquarters.

"I guessed right," Jake chuckled. "You're there. What are you doing at the office so late?"

"Oh, you know, old friend, the wheels have got to keep turning."

"I thought being president of the company meant you could hire people to roll those wheels for you."

"Old habits are hard to break. What have you found out?"

Jake shrugged away the hollow tone in George's voice. "Well, I know who has our baby."

"Who?"

"Name's Bill Clayton. Works for Worldwide in Denver."

"Our Worldwide?"

"The one and only."

A long breath of silence was suspended in

the wires that stretched over the earth from Texas to India. "What's he doing with it?"

"Kleinman and Dawson gave it to him in Frankfurt. He tried to pass it on to their contact here, but it looks like some other competition got in the way."

"Kleinman. Son of a bitch. Should have guessed. So what's with this Clayton. What does he do for Worldwide?"

Jake stuck a new cigar in his mouth and lit the end before answering. "He's the new vice-president of international taxation."

"The name's familiar. Any criminal record?"

"Clean as a whistle."

The timbre of George's voice changed, and a deepening anger billowed up. "So why don't you have it? Why does he, for God's sake!"

"I'll get it, George."

"When?"

Jake chewed methodically on the tip of the cigar. George had never doubted his ways of doing things before. What was the problem this time? "This has to be handled delicately. Clayton's with a tour group."

"Where is he now?"

"I told you, here in Delhi."

"Where?"

Jake tried to keep his own anger from rising. "At the Oberoi Intercontinental."

"I want that chip, Jake."

Jake heard and registered the panic behind the words. "I know that. I said I'd get it."

Another long pause ensued between the men. "Keep in touch," George finally said.

"Yeah, sure."

George Watterman dropped the receiver into its cradle, cutting off the connection with the other side of the world. The lights were off in his office, but he leaned back in his chair and watched the changing colors of the traffic light reflect against the wall.

That goddamn piece of silicon. It was his only hope. All his energy and effort had gone into its development. He had picked the brightest and the best—Kleinman and Dawson—may they rot in hell. They had double-crossed him! They were going to be damn sorry they did that. He was going to make sure of it. And he would have to take care of them before it got out that there were really two chips instead of one. Everything hinged on that secret. Everything.

But the first thing he had to take care of was this tax accountant, Clayton. Jake had obviously lost his touch. He'd gotten soft through the years. He would have to handle it himself.

And the first step was to contact Bill Clayton, to set up a meeting of some sort.

George leaned back in his chair, trying to loosen the tightening in his chest. *Slow down, you're going to get the chip. Slow down and stop worrying.*

Despite the repetitive reassurances, the fear of failure began to clutch at the valves of his heart. The realization of what was happening brought on more fear, more burning pain, bolting him into action. He reached in his top drawer for the bottle of nitroglycerin and slipped two tiny tablets under his tongue. Sitting back once again, he felt the calm wash over him, and the burning, clutching grip loosened. It was okay. Everything was going to be all right.

Even with the balming effect of the drug, somewhere in the back of his mind the doubts continued. He had to have the chip. He had to. It was a matter of survival. His own personal survival. He would be ruined if he didn't get it back.

"Hobble on over here and let me see that knee."

Kelly moved slowly across the room toward Bill, maintaining as much dignity as possible. "I have never hobbled in my life."

He watched as her head tilted higher and

he forced himself not to smile. "Well, you are now." He pointed to the bed. "Sit."

She did, but her expression was rebellious. "Have you ever thought of saying 'Please' or 'Would you like to sit?' or something besides these monosyllabic commands you seem bent on using with me?"

Bill stared at her blandly. "Kelly dear, would you care to sit down for a spell and shut up? How was that?"

"Wonderful," she groaned, sitting on the edge of the bed and extending her hurt leg. He squatted on his heels in front of her. "Ouch! Are you into torture too?"

He got up and headed for the bathroom, wet a washcloth, and grabbed some first-aid cream from his dobkit. "Only with young, innocent maidens that I can lure to my laborrrrratory." He curled his upper lip under as if revealing fangs, then squatted down before her again.

"Hmm," she mumbled. "It's a good thing I'm not young and innocent then."

Bill laid the warm, wet cloth over her knee and lifted his eyes to her face. "You don't look so old and jaded to me."

Her mouth tightened. "You'd be surprised."

He was aware of the tinge of bitterness in her voice, but decided not to comment on it.

He heard his own inner need to touch her as it swelled to a deafening roar in his ears. "Good," he whispered over the voice within him. "Your experience is one surprise I would love to have."

Kelly felt her pulse fluttering wildly throughout her body. Suddenly she was full of doubts again. *He's the wrong kind of man for you, Kelly. Too intimidating, too dominant. What would it take for him to become like your father?*

She kept repeating the assertions to herself, but she had trouble making them stick. The simple touch of his hand upon her knee, even through the washcloth, was enough to bar all the gates of reason, leaving her alone to fight the flooding weakness that turned her will to jelly.

Still, she had to try.. "What happened today?"

His mind stumbled over the change of topic. He wasn't sure he was ready to leave his other thoughts behind just yet. Besides that, he didn't have an answer for her question. And that fact alone was enough to switch his desire to anger.

"I don't know."

"Well, I just don't understand it," she said. "I mean, this whole thing with the chip puzzles me. How could something no larger than a newborn's thumbnail assume such importance for so many people?"

His own confusion took refuge in arrogance. "That's because you have no idea of the complexities of the computer industry. You and your simpleminded arcade games."

She swatted his hand away from her knee where he was trying to spread some cream into her scraped skin. "Just because I like to play computer games does not automatically make me a simpleton."

His expression was dubious at best.

"So what is it?" she asked. "Are you just mad because I fell and hurt myself? You're thinking I'm nothing more than a burden."

"You're not a burden," he grumbled, grabbing the tube of cream from her hands.

"Well, then, why are you so mad at me?"

He stared at her, thinking about how important she had become in his life. How could he possibly be mad at her? "I'm not mad."

"You are."

"I'm not. God, would you listen to us! We're arguing like a couple of four-year-olds." He rubbed the cream into her knee, then recapped the tube and tossed it onto the nightstand. "Look," he sighed. "I didn't anticipate what happened this afternoon. That's the problem. What if it had been me they had taken instead of Graber. What if . . ." He looked at her face, his gaze dropping by inches down to her lap and his voice, when he spoke, was very soft. "What if it had been you?" He shook his head and frowned. "I didn't anticipate any of it."

"How could you have?" she asked, feeling his pain and wanting more than anything to make it right for him.

Bill was still squatting down before her and his hands lay palm down on the mattress beside Kelly's legs. He shook his head impatiently. "I should have. I should have covered every angle. I should have this thing figured out by now."

His eyes were fastened on her leg, following the sweep of flesh to the hem of her skirt that was bunched up around the tops of her thighs. His gaze lifted to her face and his eyes grew darker, his mouth curved down a fraction at the sides. "Everything has shifted gears, Kelly. Everything. I've lost control of the situation."

Kelly reached out and placed the palm of her hand against his cheek. It was an instinctive gesture. He was so vulnerable. Maybe even more so than she was. She wanted to protect him.

"God, but you are ignorant about what is important, Bill Clayton. So what if you didn't know what was going to happen this afternoon? So what if you can't handle every little problem that arises? You can't control the rest of the world. You shouldn't expect to."

Her left hand lifted to cup the other side of his face and she felt his hand gliding slowly upward on her thigh, his fingers singeing the sensitive flesh along her leg.

Her throat constricted as his hand slid around to rest on the side of her hip under her skirt. The possessive touch activated a force that spiraled through her like a restless, impetuous wind rushing with unleashed hunger against the beating of her heart.

"Are you saying I can't control you?" There was a warm challenge in his voice.

Her fingers wound through his hair, pulling him . . . or was he merely moved upward by the powerful urges within his own body? He leaned over her as she lay back on the bed, her hands holding the back of his head, guiding him down to her waiting mouth.

"Absolutely not," she said with much more conviction in her voice than she actually felt.

When his lips covered hers, she was aware of a montage of sensations. His mouth taking possession of her parted lips, his hand massaging the back of her hip under her skirt, his body pressing upward against hers. She was alive with the red-hot current of air that murmured its life-breathing message into her flesh.

Bill's body crackled with the need he had for this woman. Her body under his stirred up emotions he hadn't even known he had. He wanted her and he wanted to believe at this moment that she was his. That he really did have control over her. But he knew it was he who was lost. He who needed her mouth and her hands and her body. At this moment he was hers.

He fought to hide this new vulnerability. "I thought women wanted to be dominated." His tongue moved along her lips in deliciously slow circles.

"What gave you that crazy notion?" Her voice was nothing more than an uneven whisper.

His mouth moved down her neck in a silent, slow, sliding caress, and her hands began to pull the shirttail from the waistband of his slacks.

He slid higher on Kelly's body and she arched into him, sending a thousand needles hurtling through his veins. He'd never wanted anyone as much as he wanted her—it was crazy, it was dizzying, it was inevitable.

She felt his fingers on the clasp of her skirt, but her hands closed around his to stop him. She was frightened of this overwhelming need she had for him. Was that what had happened to her mother? Had her spirit been crushed with the same compelling passion?

Bill felt the tightening of her body and knew it had nothing to do with desire. Something had scared her. What had he done?

He looked down at her eyes; they were filled with a pain he could not understand. "What's the matter?"

"This is wrong for me."

His hands lay on either side of her head as he leaned over her. "What is wrong about it?" he asked, frustration underscoring the attempt to understand.

Kelly flattened her palms against his chest, unconsciously holding him at bay. "It . . . it is this problem I have."

"What kind of problem?"

"I feel out of control and that . . . that scares me." Her eyes pleaded with him to understand. "You overwhelm me so, and that is something that I've never been able to handle in a relationship before."

"If that wasn't so absurd, I might laugh, Kelly. You're out of control! You have more control than any other woman I've ever known! There is no reason for you to feel that way. I know that I came on a little strong when we first met, but . . ."

"It's not you, Bill. It's me. It is my problem, and I have to deal with it in my own way."

He studied her eyes and then her mouth. His fingers pulled a strand of her hair to the side and he smiled. "How long is that going to take?"

She couldn't hold back the smile. He looked so eager to change her mind, so trustworthy and boyish. "Maybe not very long at all."

The sound of the phone beside them gave a final puncture to the sensual air that had enveloped them only moments before. Bill glared at the phone. But before answering, he kissed Kelly's neck. "We'll continue this . . . conversation in a minute."

He grabbed the phone in irritation. "Yes," he growled, taking out his frustration on the unfortunate party at the other end of the line.

"Bill Clayton, please. Hold for a call from America."

"Bill Clayton?" The male voice came across the wires clearly.

"Yes?"

"My name is George Watterman. I'm president of Lambert Technologies."

"Yes," Bill said. Of course he knew who George Watterman was. And, having read a hundred of Lambert's annual reports, he even had the face to put with the voice. Well, good, now at least he would get some answers.

He watched Kelly sit up on the bed and straighten her clothes. When he noticed her wet eyes, something sharp and painful plunged into his chest. In one swift movement he grabbed her and pulled her next to him, wrapping his arm tightly around her waist.

"I understand you have something that belongs to my company," George said, drawing Bill's concentration back to the phone.

His eyes narrowed in thought before he answered. "I'm not sure whom it belongs to."

"Why is that?" George's voice was strong but toneless.

"I've been getting some conflicting stories."

"Such as?"

Bill glanced at Kelly and absently ran his thumb up and down her arm. "Why don't you just tell me what the chip is to be used for?" he said.

The reply was several beats of silence. "Look, Bill. I'll tell you what. Why don't we cut out all the middlemen—"

"In other words, get rid of all your goons who have been tracking me?"

George ignored the interruption. "Let's just make this thing between you and me. We can meet, talk, you can tell me how much you want for the safe return of the chip. Everything will be worked out fine. What do you say?"

How much I want? Bill thought. *The president of one of the largest corporations in the world is going to pay me to get his chip back? That doesn't make sense. Why doesn't he just call in the law?*

Bill's body tensed and his fingers circled Kelly's arm tightly. It was a trap. The man was setting him up for something.

"Sure, we can meet somewhere," he said cautiously, "but you obviously are aware that I'm on the opposite side of the world."

"That's no problem. I can be there in two days."

"We won't be here," Bill delighted in saying.

"Where will you be?"

He paused, enjoying every second he could make George Watterman squirm. He no longer thought he was going to get the answers he wanted. This man was out to get him just like everyone else seemed to be right now. "Bombay."

"All right," George answered slowly. "Where will you be staying?"

"Where will you be staying?" Bill asked, caution taking over where trust ended.

George thought for a minute. "At the Taj."

"Fine." Bill started to hang up the phone.

"Wait!" George's voice boomed across the line. "Where will we meet? How will I contact you?"

"You won't. I'll contact you." With that, Bill cradled the phone, ending the conversation that both disconcerted him and, at the same time, wrapped him in a cloak of raw power.

Only when he looked back at Kelly still in his arms, her gray eyes revealing the desires and the secrets and the frustration that clung to them both, did he realize how powerless he was to define what was happening in his life.

He had thought he could manage this without her; assumed he could handle it all on his own. But he now knew that despite his inability to fully understand what she was beginning to mean to him he needed her in his life.

He expelled a drawn-out breath of resignation and rested his chin on the top of her head. "Kelly, I need your help."

She watched him closely, wanting to believe that he needed more than just her help.

"Please," he added, and she closed her eyes and rested her head against his shoulder. The warmth of his skin penetrated the shirt and caressed her cheek, and she knew for now that this was enough.

CHAPTER TEN

Much like her feelings for Bill, India was a paradox to Kelly. It was a stench, it was the fragrance of jasmine; it was a strength of spirit, it was a denial of spirit; it was a sickness, and it was a testament to life.

Kelly stood before the Taj Mahal, in its splendid white purity interlaced with colorful, semi-precious stones. As she stared up at this greatest of monuments to love and to the enduring strength of the unbeatable human spirit, she felt the contradictions within her own life.

She watched as a barefoot brown girl of four or five wearing a tattered dress meandered shyly toward her, stopping ten feet away. She squatted down and picked a flower, holding it out to Kelly in an unspoken invitation.

Kelly smiled and raised her camera. With the little girl framed by the backdrop of the Taj Mahal, in all its rich splendor, she captured the spirit of the country in one shot.

She handed a rupee to the child and stared after her as the girl ran off, clutching the money in her tiny fist, her fate ruled by the rigid social stratification that allowed no individual spirit to rise above its destiny.

Kelly had never known poverty, and yet she had never known a spiritual richness of life either. Would she, in contrast to the little girl, be able to rise above her past, overcome the fate that had ruled her life with its iron fist? She closed her eyes, thinking of the almost painful need she had for Bill Clayton, wishing that dependency would go away but suspecting that it would not.

She didn't want to feel this need for him. It reminded her too much of her mother. She had married a man who needed to assert his dominance with every breath. It had taken away her profession, and had crushed whatever spirit and drive and individualism her mother ever had.

That was what Kelly was afraid of. That was what she didn't want Bill to do to her.

She watched him as he climbed the steps to the Taj Mahal and stopped to marvel at the exquisite craftsmanship evident in every stone of the edifice. The long rectangular pool of water that lay before it reflected the sun at its zenith. And all around the grounds and the building were women in their long saris, barefoot and brown, their bodies and heads draped in yards of bright, colorful cloth.

Kelly kept her camera clicking almost continuously as she tried to capture the symmetrical beauty of this country's most cherished monument.

When she finally lowered her camera, she looked up to the top of the stairs and saw Bill watching her, a half smile playing upon his lips. She climbed the stairs to join him.

"What are you grinning about?" she asked.

"There's an empty bench over there. I just didn't want you to forget that."

She dutifully lifted her camera and shot one frame of the bench. "Satisfied?"

His smile changed shape and his eyes matched the glow of the lapis stones in the monument. "Not yet," he said. "But I hope I will be soon."

The bus ride to Agra had been a long four hours, but the ride back to Delhi was interminable. Hot and tired from the day-long excursion, Bill rested his head against the seat back and thought about how nice a shower and a cold beer would be right now.

Kelly was sitting in the seat beside him, but she was jotting down notes for her article in a small notebook, so he contented himself with watching her while she worked.

He felt full of her. The way she bent her head, the way she held a pencil, the way she draped a sweater around her shoulders so casually. She consumed his every thought. And he didn't know what to do about it. Would these crazy feelings go away on their own? He just didn't know.

He tried to force his thoughts away from her and instead watched the countryside roll by outside the window. They passed village after village that served as constant reminders to Bill of how much Americans take for granted. Villagers slept in the sun and relieved themselves on the side of the road. Tiny naked children carried even tinier naked tots in their arms while their mothers and fathers worked the fields. A Double Up Cola advertisement touting *Double Up for the Good Life* hung on the side of a small hovel that housed five or six families.

Behind Bill and Kelly, Mrs. Willard was sound asleep as she had been since they left Delhi early this morning. Her niece, Muffy, and Damien Brewster were making the most of their time together in the back of the bus. And Mr. Fowler leaned over to Winfred Rotterborg and began detailing the innumerable technical faults of the latest Mideast peace settlement.

Bill listened to the three widows chirping at the front of the bus with the guide and cringed every time he heard another one of their questions.

"What are those lovely little flowers alongside the road, Mr. Angelique?"

Angel's stammering reply was as idiotic as the question. "Why I do not know, ladies, but I believe they brighten the little village so much, no?"

Bill closed his eyes in disgust, only to open them again and find "E.T." looking at him.

"I think Professor Evanston likes you," Kelly whispered, glancing up to catch Bill's grimace.

"Just what I need right now, a gay extraterrestrial professor, and your razzing."

"Just trying to cheer you up a bit," she smiled.

"I know it sounds terrible, but I've gotten to the point where I don't trust anyone. Even the people on this tour."

"I know what you mean," Kelly said. "They look like real suspicious characters."

Bill glanced at her to see if her remark was intended as facetiously as it sounded. Her grin was positively wicked.

He shook his head and laughed. "Hell, I'm even beginning to distrust the sweet little old Caldwells."

Kelly looked at him with disbelief. "You are paranoid!"

By the time the bus pulled up in front of the hotel, everyone on the tour was so sick of the ride and each other's company that they scurried into the cool interior of the lobby as quickly as possible. Bill held the glass door to the foyer open for Kelly, but she bypassed him and walked to the edge of the sidewalk to hail a taxi.

He reached out for her arm. "Where are you going?"

"Old Delhi."

Angel's gasp intruded upon the scene. "What! Why you want to go to Old Delhi? We leaving for Bombay dis afternoon."

Kelly planted her hands on her hips. "Because it's there, Angel. Because it's there." She started to open the door to the cab, but Bill planted his body in front of her.

"You can't go alone to Old Delhi," he insisted.

"The tour is not going there," she answered with equal insistence.

His jaw slackened in challenge. "So you're just going to go tripping off by yourself, right?"

"Something like that. Any objections?"

Angel edged his way into the discussion with a placating tone. "Miss Kelly . . ."

Bill hovered over her. "Plenty," he growled, not allowing Angel even the space to breathe, much less speak. "First of all, you could go in there and never reappear. Second of all . . ." He turned and glowered at Angel, waiting impatiently for the guide to disappear.

Angel shrugged repeatedly and backed away, hurrying into the hotel to take care of the rest of his flock.

"Second of all," Bill continued, "after all that has been happening in the last few days, I can't believe you would go off by yourself anywhere."

She crossed her arms and looked away. "I need time to think."

Bill stared at her as if she were daft. "You can think in your room." Time to think had been robbed from him in the last couple of days. He was reacting on pure gut instinct now. "You're not going to Old Delhi alone."

Kelly's mouth tightened as she glared at Bill. She certainly was not intimidated by him! Who did he think he was anyway! Her shoulders sagged a bit as she thought of his hands running along her thighs, his mouth so warm and moist against her own. "You're right, I guess."

"Good." He breathed easier. "Now, let's go into the hotel and get out of this heat. I'm—"

"You can come along," she decided, smiling as she watched his jaw drop in disbelief.

He slowly shook his head. "Damn, but you're a conniving woman."

As if driving from day into night, the taxi moved at a snail's pace under the ancient archway that led into the old part of the city. Where New Delhi was wide avenues with earth-colored government buildings and flower-bedecked Victorian homes, Old Delhi was a collage of festering filth. Emaciated chickens squawked in cages that were piled ten high, and the smell of chutney and onions and dung and dirt pervaded every molecule of air. It clung to everyone and everything. And especially here, it was laden with the horrid stench of poverty. It was a smell Kelly would never forget as long as she lived.

She tapped the driver on the shoulder to stop the taxi. "I want to walk."

"I don't think that's such a good idea," Bill said.

She turned to him, exasperated. "How can

you say you've seen India when you haven't seen this?"

"I can see it just fine from the inside of a taxi," Bill said, but paid the driver anyway and opened his door.

The sky above them was clear and bright, but for some reason it seemed dark and overcast where they walked. Scrawny dogs and scrawny children played together in the streets while the parents scampered about in a frenzied dance of survival, buying chickens and fruit at the markets, carrying water from community wells, beating rugs against the sides of buildings to rid them of dust, or pulling a wagon with all of their possessions to a new location.

While they walked, Kelly took photographs, housing the impressions and images in her mind as well as on film. "Have you decided yet how you're going to handle George Watterman?"

"I have a plan . . . sort of."

Kelly's mouth twisted sideways. "In which you're not going to include me?"

He smiled at her. "You're included. In fact, you're the go-between."

Her eyes widened excitedly as she listened to his plans for meeting with George. Bill noticed her expression, and tried to warn her not to see this as some sort of game. But he wasn't sure she really even heard him. Damn, he thought, she looked so sweet at times like this, almost childlike in her glee. Her hands were clasped in front of her and her gray eyes were wide and innocent.

He laid his hand behind her head and pulled her close, letting her soft, happy smile warm his lips. But when he rested his chin on the top of her head, his eyes locked with those of two men—Kleinman and Dawson. The two men from Lambert who had given him the chip in Frankfurt were now following him along the streets of Old Delhi. When they realized he had spotted them, they ducked into a low doorway. But the damage was done. He had seen them.

He put his arm around Kelly and they once again started moving down the winding streets.

"You're gripping my arm too tight." Kelly frowned up at him. "And you're walking too fast."

They turned right at the next corner. "There are a couple of men following us. The men from Lambert. Please, don't fall apart on me."

She yanked her arm free and glared at him for one hostile moment before resuming her step.

Bill gritted his teeth, cursing himself for the

foolish remark. "I'm sorry, Kelly." He took hold of her hand and squeezed it gently. "I didn't mean that."

She sighed. "You did mean it, Bill. You still think I'm some dumb broad who can't even take care of myself, much less you."

He stopped and turned her by the shoulders, holding her there in front of him. "Listen, do me a favor and don't stop trying to drill it into my head, okay?"

It was an admission of need, she knew. And it was probably the best she was going to get out of this man for now, so she nodded. "Don't worry, I won't give up. You're a challenge. Are they still following?"

He looked behind them again, searching every shadow and doorway for the two men dressed so conspicuously in western clothes. But all he saw were women draped in yards of black cloth and men in ragged shirts and pants shuffling down the street in an unending pursuit of life.

Bill and Kelly maintained an even pace, trying to keep a perspective on where they were and where the exit to the new part of the city was. They had to get on the other side of the archway before they would ever find a taxi. Certainly none would be driving through here looking for passengers. They had to reach New Delhi.

"Bill, look!" Kelly pointed to the two men. She shivered and inched her body closer to his. "We're in trouble, aren't we?"

"'Fraid so, darlin'." He tried to keep his voice light, but he hadn't fooled her. She knew somehow that they had stepped into a danger for which neither of them was prepared.

"What do we do?"

"I hate to use an old cliché, but we run for our lives." He had no way of knowing whether they had guns or not, but he wasn't about to take a chance. They would have to outrun them.

"Oh, my God, Bill, look! They're right behind us and . . . I think they have guns!"

He wouldn't let them use them. He was not going to let Kelly or himself die on the streets of Old Delhi, ten thousand miles away from home. They were going to survive.

With his arm about her waist, they dashed across the street at an angle, darting around a horsedrawn cart and heading for the next block, which they hoped was near the arch. They rounded the corner, almost running head-on into an old woman carrying a huge clay jug of water on top of her head.

He heard his feet pounding against the dirt-covered street, heard the lighter sound of Kelly's feet next to him. They didn't look back; they simply ran. Kelly felt the blood bounding through her veins and in her temples, felt the heat and fear that clung to her body as she kept up with Bill. Life surged through her.

As they neared the archway, Bill slowed enough to look behind them. The two men were still following, but they obviously were not in great shape and Bill knew that he and Kelly could get to a taxi before the men reached them. He gripped Kelly's arm more tightly and the two of them ran to safety.

They clung to each other in the hotel room, aware of every breath and every pulse that beat between them. They were safe. For the moment they were safe, and that was all that mattered. That and the feel of each other's arms reaffirming that they were alive.

Nothing was said between them, for the frantic movement of their hands and the abandoned searching of their mouths said it all.

Kelly's thoughts were concentrated solely upon this man with whom she had barely escaped death. Together they had conquered their foe. Together nothing would be impossible.

Bill pressed her against the door of his room, holding her body pinioned between the hard wood and his equally hard body. His hands were entwined with hers, holding them prisoner at the sides of her head. His mouth possessed her, controlled and dominated every fiber of her being. But this time she opened herself to it, letting him in, wanting his total possession, wanting to give him all that he needed from her.

Bill was full of power, full of the invincibility that this woman built in him. He no longer could hold back his emotions with her. He was hers. And together they would take on the world.

His tongue probed deeper, the buttons of his shirt pressing against her breasts, his body lifting her, arching against her. There was no softness, no tenderness. There was only his body demanding everything from hers. And everything was what she wanted to give.

His lips moved fervently across her face, down around the back of her neck beneath her hair. One of her hands was freed when he tangled his fingers into her hair, cradling the back of her head in his huge grasp. His breath was like a windstorm near her ear, ragged, full of the rage of life.

Her free hand clutched at his back, then slid down to his jean-clad hips, urging him tighter against her. His hand slipped down between their bodies and tugged at the buttons of her blouse, wrenching two of them loose to fly across the room. His fingers grasped her breast with that same overpowering intensity, and Kelly knew a rush of desire that she had never known before.

He pulled back enough to quickly remove her blouse and bra, flinging them onto the floor, his gaze piercing her with all the dark intensity of his feelings. Her skirt and panties were discarded with the same careless dispatch. And then she watched him yank his own garments off, adding them to the pile of discarded clothing on the floor.

Pressing her back to the door with his hands, he lowered himself enough to cover her breasts with his mouth. His tongue raked across her flesh like a trail of fire, leaving behind burning wreckage in its wake. Her fingers were in his hair, guiding him from one breast to the other, her moans punctuating each stroke of his tongue and teeth.

His mouth dropped down to stroke the fuller part of her abdomen, and the exquisite torture continued until she cried his name into the air.

Immediately he was in front of her, still pressing her against the door. "Kelly? Is it all right?" His breath was labored and quick.

"Yes, don't worry about . . . oh, please!"

This time his hardened flesh moved between her legs, pushing up, expanding her inner self, filling her with the power of flesh uniting in passion.

"Bill . . ." she cried again when he lifted her higher against the door, impaling her with his body. He buried his tongue deep inside her mouth.

She felt some interior shell expanding, growing larger, unfurling until it at last erupted into a thousand shattering parts, each of which was flung into the air where it cascaded down in a shower of simmering debris. Before all the pieces reached the ground, she felt Bill's body follow the same explosive path as hers.

They leaned against the door, weak and exhausted, and it was a couple of minutes before he pulled back enough to look down at her. "Are you okay?" He still had to struggle for breath.

She nodded. "I think so."

He watched her carefully, wanting to know what she was thinking and feeling. "I didn't hurt you, did I?"

"No," she said, but tears sprang to her eyes.

Immediately Bill lifted her in his arms and carried her to the bed, laying her down gently on top of the covers. He lay beside her, partially covering her body with his own. "Kelly?" He wiped away a few stray tears. "You'd tell me if I hurt you, wouldn't you?"

"You didn't hurt me, Bill. It felt . . . wonderful. It just scared me a little."

It was the first time he had ever really cared about how a woman felt afterward. He wasn't even sure what he was supposed to say or do. But with Kelly he wanted to try. It wasn't enough just to possess her body. He wanted to know her, feel her, care for her. "It scares the hell out of me too," he said.

He kissed her gently this time and his fingers ran through the length of her hair, pulling it to the sides, where it fanned out from her face. "Why does it scare you?"

She looked into the depths of those blue eyes, so open now, allowing a clear path into the part of him that had been closed to her before. She wanted to tell him, wanted him to know it all, but she couldn't make the words come out right. "Dominant men have always frightened me a little," she finally admitted. "No, not a little. A lot."

Bill watched her closely, thinking of all the things she'd said before, the clues and hints into her background. He had pushed it all aside, not really wanting to know, wanting to keep her as nothing more substantial than a sexual object, a plaything. But as he looked into her moist gray eyes and noticed the tiny quiver in her lips, he could no longer do that with her. She was different from all the others. For the first time in his life he wanted to be a part of a woman's existence and to know her as completely as he knew himself.

"You said once before that your father bullied you. Is that what you mean by dominant?"

She nodded, not sure she really wanted to say much more about it. She had already revealed so much of herself, leaving the wounds exposed for more hurt. Fear of that hurt now kept her quiet.

He saw the tightening of her lips and knew she didn't want to talk about it. But he had come this far; he wasn't going to back off now. "What did he do that scared you so?"

She shook her head, stalling for time. "He made my mother miserable. He forced her to give up her career, controlled every move she made, criticized anything she ever did, until finally she just gave up. She sort of . . . caved in, until there was nothing there. Just an empty space. All the life had been squeezed out of her."

"And you're afraid the same thing might happen to you?" Bill asked, once again stroking her hair and the side of her face with his fingers.

178

"It could." She looked at him closely, wanting him to deny it, but knowing he wouldn't.

"But you're not the same as your mother. Just because he dominated her doesn't mean you can be dominated as easily. Maybe she was a weaker woman than you are." The words came thoughtfully, and yet Bill never heard them in his own mind. It never occurred to him that that same advice might apply to him. "Besides," he smiled, "who could possibly presume to control you? You're one of the strongest women I know."

"I wasn't so strong a while ago."

"What do you mean?"

She looked embarrassed. "I mean when we were . . ."

"Ah, locked in heavenly transport."

She caught the twinkle in his eyes and grinned. "Plastered against the door was more like it."

He shrugged. "Okay, plastered against the door. Not quite as romantic-sounding, but an apt description nevertheless. So what's the problem? You didn't like it?"

He knew better than that, and so did she. She thumped his chest with her fist. "I didn't say that."

He shifted her so she was cradled in his arms. "I'm waiting for your answer."

She felt a flood of weakness attack her mid-

179

section when he fit himself against her. She closed her eyes, sighing. "I love the feel of your body, Bill. I love the things, all the things you do to me. It's just that . . ."

"Just what?" he whispered.

"I'm afraid I won't know where the line is between dominance and violence."

He frowned at her. "You think I might turn violent?"

"No. . . . I don't know. I . . ."

"Have other men been violent with you?"

"There haven't been that many men in my life," she hedged.

"You didn't answer my question." He stared down at her, watching every move of her mouth and eyes. "Was your father violent?"

She quickly looked away and swallowed convulsively. "It was mostly verbal abuse. He didn't want me around much. But, yes, sometimes he hit me."

Bill closed his eyes. It was a long minute before he could look over at her again. "What did your mother do about it?"

Kelly tried to laugh. "Nothing. It's funny in a way. She just wasn't there most of the time. I mean her body was there, but . . . well, it was like knocking at her door and she wouldn't answer. You knew she was in there, but she wouldn't open the door." Kelly sighed. "She wouldn't open it and you wondered what it was you'd done."

He moved over her now, his hands caressing her jaw as his mouth slowly dipped down to hers. It was a gentle kiss, soft and tender, and full of an understanding she'd thought him incapable of. He raised himself up only slightly. "Kelly, I don't want to hurt you. All I want to do is make love with you and make you feel very very good. Don't let that scare you."

She watched him hungrily, wanting his touch, his mouth, his loving. "I won't," she breathed, pulling him down to her waiting body. "I won't."

CHAPTER ELEVEN

Edgar Dawson stuffed another bite of Bombay chicken into his mouth. He debated on whether to take a swig of tap water to wash it down but, considering what country he was in, wisely decided not to. He'd just wait for room service to bring some more beer.

Klaus Kleinman sat across the makeshift table, silently devouring a curried seafood dish. Edgar grimaced as he looked at the unfamiliar food.

At the knock on the door both men jumped and dropped their forks.

"That will be room service," Kleinman said shakily.

"Yes." Dawson rose from his chair and

walked to the door. He slid the chain loose, then unbolted the lock and turned the handle.

The door was opened with one powerful shove.

Dawson and Kleinman stared with wide eyes and gaping mouths as George Watterman stepped into the room, then slowly closed the door and latched it.

The three men were enveloped in a silent sweat for several long seconds.

George finally broke the silence. "Well, well, here we are again. The three of us behind closed doors. Secret meetings, if you will." He walked about the room, casually surveying the furniture. "You hadn't planned on this part of it, had you?"

The two men stared at George across the room, both wishing they'd never come up with this crazy scheme in the first place. But they had thought it would be so simple, so easy.

"You see," George said, walking to the table and picking up a piece of chicken, tasting it, then tossing it back onto the plate. "When I picked you two to work on this project, it was because I knew you were the best computer engineers around."

The two men sat up straighter in their

chairs, relief washing through them at the unexpected compliment.

"I must say, though, I didn't expect you to take such initiative and just whisk my pride and joy out from under me."

Their faces fell.

"Why didn't you come to me, tell me you wanted a cut of the action?"

"What would you have said if we had?" Dawson asked.

George smiled, but it never carried over to his eyes. "I'm sure I would have told you to go to hell," he laughed. "But then, it never hurts to try, does it?"

Kleinman looked over at Dawson and shrugged. "Are you saying you might want to make a deal now?"

"What's there to deal with? You don't have the chip. You gave it away."

"We only gave it to this guy to carry to Delhi for us. Our contact there was to pick it up."

Dawson glanced with sharp warning at Kleinman, but the other man didn't notice.

"And your contact, what was he going to do with it?"

"He was to meet with someone from Rider," Kleinman said.

"Rider Instruments? The Japanese firm?"

"That's the one."

"They offered a hell of a lot for that little chip, George."

"I'm sure they did, Klaus," he said as if speaking to a child. "I'm sure they did. However . . ." He shook his head and paused before going on. "There are two problems with your little plan."

"Yeah?"

"Yeah. Number one, Bill Clayton has the chip and I don't think he has any intention of giving it back for free. I don't want him to find out what it really is. Because if he finds out, everyone else in the company would find out and"—he smiled menacingly—"that would be a disaster for me, now, wouldn't it?"

Kleinman cleared his throat. "What's the other problem?"

"I did say there were two, didn't I?" George smiled and looked from one man to the other. "The second problem—and what you might consider your . . . fatal mistake—is that you double-crossed me."

Kelly stood outside the luxurious hotel in Bombay and took several deep breaths to calm her jittery nerves. She wiped her sweaty palms against the blue cotton of her peasant skirt, then readjusted the shoulder strap of her straw bag, little movements that minimized the butterflies of excitement that flew wild and free inside her stomach.

Straightening her shoulders and swallowing the last drops of fear, she walked through the glass doors into the lobby of the Taj. The cool marble floor and bubbling fountain, its clear spray scintillating in the natural light of the foyer, was a stark contrast to the hot arid world that existed outside these walls.

Industrious sikhs, bearded and turbaned, conducted business affairs over cups of tea, while wealthy wives, draped in silk saris and fashionable churidar kurtas, sat idly by, mere accessories in their men's lives.

Outside the luxury of the hotel the rest of Bombay was teeming with infested slums, where over half of its million residents lived.

Kelly scanned the lobby until she spotted George Watterman standing exactly where Bill had instructed him to be. He was to stand to the left of the fountain with a *Wall Street Journal* folded vertically in his right hand.

Kelly smiled to herself as she remembered Bill commanding George over the phone: "I don't care if you have to fly all the way back to Dallas to find one. You will have a *Wall Street Journal* in your hand!"

She was still amazed at the way Bill had handled the situation. He had thought of every detail, forgetting nothing, covering every angle. They had spent the entire day yesterday studying Bombay and the hotel for the best place to meet the president of Lambert Technologies.

She wondered if George Watterman had even the faintest idea of the kind of man he was up against. Kelly knew it was going to be an interesting confrontation, to say the least.

George wasn't expecting a woman to show up, so Kelly hung back for a moment, studying him. It was a perfect opportunity to assess this person who had control over so many people and so much money.

He was bulky but, despite his excess weight, his face revealed a steeliness that most likely carried over to his body. He was rough-cut, from a mold that belied the clean-cut, corporate-president tradition.

Making one last minor adjustment to her clothing, Kelly walked up to the man. "Hello."

George cast a casual glance at her, revealing an insignificant amount of interest.

Kelly wanted to smile. "My name is Kelly."

"That's nice," he muttered. "But listen, honey, I'm not interested in any afternoon rendezvous, okay?"

This time she did smile. "No, I'm sure you're not." She marveled at her own ability to remain calm despite the bundle of nerves that coiled and snaked like live wires through her body. "However, I did hear that your company was interested in computer technology."

George's head snapped around and his eyes narrowed on her with new interest. "Where did you hear that?"

"Oh, from a friend of mine." Kelly studied one of her fingernails closely. "Of course, you probably haven't heard of him. I mean the whole world is obsessed with this computer business and . . ."

"Bill Clayton?"

Her expression was one of veritable shock. "What a small world it is! That happens to be the name of my friend."

George's expression hardened around the edges. "He was supposed to meet me."

Kelly looped her arm through the man's, once again applauding her consummate acting ability. "Shall we go?"

"Where are we going?"

"Don't worry, Mr. Watterman. I know the way."

George glared into the hot sun as they left the hotel, hating the blindness that was enveloping him at this moment. He detested this helpless feeling of not knowing what was going on. Who in hell was this girl and what was her part in Clayton's scheme? Well, he'd

188

go along for a little while anyway. He really had no choice. But if things got out of hand, he would hold the last card. Just as he had with Kleinman and Dawson. They would cause him no more problems, that was for sure. It was just a crying shame that they wouldn't be around to use all of that incredible computer knowledge.

As if to emphasize in his own mind the power he would wield over Bill Clayton and this girl, George let his hand drop to the pocket of his slacks, where the small pistol lay in wait. His fingers closed around the grip, the pearl handle and steel shaft reassuring him with their cold power.

They climbed into the back of a taxi and Kelly directed the driver to the Chor Bazaar on Mutton Street. She had turned her head away from him, looking out her side of the car, so he didn't try to initiate any conversation. He would find out all he needed to know in a few minutes. And then Bill Clayton would be sorry he'd ever seen that damn chip.

The taxi wound through the city, past public buildings in the Indo-Gothic style and past a burning ghat where Hindus cremated their dead. The driver slammed on the car's brakes continually and leaned on the horn as the taxi wove in and out of the throngs of people and cars that battled for space in the streets.

George glared with abhorrence at the beggars who clung to the side of the car every time they slowed down. Eyes staring out from emaciated faces and bodies. He'd seen them all over the world. India didn't have any corner on the hunger market.

He had come a long way from his own humbler beginnings, and he didn't like being reminded of them. Being in places like this just made him sick.

To reaffirm his own motto of survival of the fittest, he took note of every TV antenna that protruded from the roof of a hovel, counted the women who emerged from darkened doorways wearing gold necklaces, and observed the businessmen who, wearing immaculate suits and carrying briefcases, made their way through the masses of humanity. He purposefully turned away from the little children who ran alongside the car and from a thin, dry woman who, holding an infant in her arms, placed her hand against the window in beseechment. He wasn't going to give them a dime.

God, he hated this place!

Bill leaned against the side of a building, keeping his eye trained on the corner where Kelly was to get out of the taxi. When she finally arrived with George, Bill straightened away from the wall, taking several deep breaths to steady the racing of his own pulse.

Kelly looked over at him and he nodded. She looped her arm in George's and led him down the sidewalk toward Bill.

Bill stepped in front of them and felt a thin film of icy sweat trickle down his spine when he saw the cold look of hate on the president's face. What if he were wrong about this? This was the president of his parent company. What was going to happen to his career after this?

Expelling a quick breath, Bill eased into the plan he had set in motion two days ago. "Glad you could join us," he said to George.

"I'm not going to waste my time or yours, Clayton. I want that—"

"Let's walk." Stepping beside George, Bill led the three of them down the street, interrupting any of George's further remarks by pointing out things of interest in the marketplace.

"Thought this was a fitting place for us to meet," Bill said. "Chor Bazaar. The name means Thieves' Market." He felt the sudden flash of George's eyes on him and knew he'd struck a nerve.

He had to keep digging for the most sensitive hollows he could find in the man. Somewhere inside of him the truth about the chip was buried. And Bill was going to learn that truth. He was tired of being toyed with. He would wait, bide his time until Watterman was ready to give him all the information he wanted.

"Interesting city, Bombay." Bill tried to dig deeper into Watterman's hard casing. "It's a city out of control, strangling on its own prosperity. Look at this." He picked up a fake Gucci purse that lay jumbled on a table with dozens of other replicas. "Nothing is real anymore."

George looked at the purse, then at Bill. "Progress is real, Clayton. Beyond that there is nothing."

"Progress." Bill tasted the word on his tongue. "Is that what this is all about? The reason you've sent your henchmen after me? This chip represents progress?"

"That and money."

"How much money?"

"That depends on who's buying it."

"And if you're buying it?"

"I'm not. I'm selling it." A guarded look fell across George's face. He had said too much. Bill saw this and stored away the information. George Watterman wanted to sell the chip. To the government maybe?

Bill shook his head slowly. "You can't sell it if you don't have it."

"I plan to have it."

"Not if you don't answer my questions."

"Such as?"

"What kind of chip is it? What's it to be used for?"

George's head snapped up, his brow creased in speculation over Bill's question. There was a trace of wonder in his voice. "You really don't know, do you?"

"I didn't steal the thing from your company, Watterman. It was given to me by two men who claimed to work for you."

George nodded, then stared at Bill for a long moment before glancing at Kelly, who was waiting expectantly. "It's what is called an artificial intelligence chip."

Bill searched the man's face, looking for any hint of a lie. So far he saw none. "And?"

"What that means is that scientists—we call them knowledge engineers—interview other scientists, doctors, experts in certain fields. They tease from them as much factual knowledge as they can, as well as the unrecognized rules of thumb they use to apply the knowledge. What we do then is encode that information on PROMs, that is, programmable read only memory, then implant them into more comprehensive programs where the computer can then deduce problems, diagnose diseases, formulate the structure of molecules, or whatever."

"Is Lambert the first company to construct these?"

"No, but we'll be the first in the market with a program like the one we've developed. This is war, Clayton. Whether people want to believe it or not is beside the point. Japan and America are at war."

"They don't have anything on the market like this?"

"Not yet. And I don't intend for them to beat us to it either."

"Progress." Bill sniffed deprecatingly, then glanced up at Kelly and smiled. From another table he picked up a small statue of a man with an elephant's head. "Ganesh," he said to George, holding up the statue. "Bombay's favorite god, the Hindu lord of prosperity and wisdom."

There was a round of silence among the three people.

Bill finally broke the quiet. "How do I know you're not lying to me, Watterman?"

"Trust."

Bill laughed, deep and full. "Trust. That's a good one." He laughed again before setting steady eyes on the man. "I've always been a trusting person, George. But in the last few days I've learned to trust no one."

They all watched one another closely, tension flowing between them like a river full of thick sludge.

"I'm not going to give you the chip, Watterman." Bill watched the shock spread across the man's face. "Not until I have this thing checked out by someone, someone who doesn't have a stake in whatever it represents. If you're telling me the truth, I'll make sure you get it back. If you're lying . . ."

The sentence hung in the air for a long, stiff minute while the two men's eyes locked in deadly confrontation. Before either Kelly or Bill realized what was happening, George locked an arm around Kelly's waist and pressed the still-pocketed gun against her back.

"I'm through playing your little games, Clayton. Now we play by my rules."

Bill felt the skin tighten along the back of his neck and he watched the shadows of panic darken Kelly's face. He had tried to warn her that the danger for them was not over. And he had known deep inside that he shouldn't involve her in this. But she had insisted and he had needed her beside him. He had wanted her to be a part of his life.

If anything happened to her, he'd never forgive himself. Never.

"Give me the chip, Clayton. Now."

Without another moment's hesitation, Bill reached into his shirt pocket and extracted the small black case that housed the quarter-inch fleck of silicon. He held it in his hands, turning it over a couple of times between his fingers.

Bill placed a possessive hand on Kelly's arm, pulling her toward him at the same moment he handed the ceramic case to George. The two men continued to stare at each other for a moment longer. Then George turned and made his way back through the crowds of the Chor Bazaar, losing himself in a backdrop as desperate as the force that brought him halfway around the world.

The return in a taxi to Chowpatty Beach was a long, silent ride. Only when they drew near the hotel did Kelly speak.

"I didn't know he had a gun." Her voice was soft and full of wonder. She hadn't expected that kind of action from the president of a major corporation.

"Enough excitement for you?" Bill asked, his voice tinged with frustration.

Kelly frowned at Bill. What was the matter with him? It was as if he resented her all of a sudden; the old cynicism was creeping back into his voice. But she tried to brush away the remark. "Well, I guess we're out of the picture now."

Bill glanced at her sharply. "Not necessarily." He hesitated for a second, then lifted the tail of his shirt, revealing a tiny square taped to his side.

Kelly stared, dumbstruck. "What is that?"

"The chip."

"But . . . you gave George . . . What did you give George?"

"I gave him one off a circuit board that goes to my office in Bangkok."

"Why?"

"Why!" Bill's tone was now one of exasperation. "Because I wasn't about to give him the right one. Not until I know for sure that the chip is what he says it is."

"But he pulled a gun on me."

"That's exactly why I had to give him a substitute. The man, or the company, is up to something, and I'm going to find out what."

"But didn't it concern you that he held a gun to my back? What if he had known that the chip you gave him was a fake?"

Concern me! Concern me! Bill looked the other way and took a deep breath. When he had seen that gun pressed against her side, it was as if his whole life were on the line. He had thought of nothing but her. How could she not know that! When he finally spoke, his voice was low and hoarse. "God damn it, Kelly, I told you this wasn't a game. I warned you that there could be danger."

"Then why didn't you include me in this little scheme of yours? I deserve to know what's going on. This is supposed to be a team effort."

He was getting in too deep with her—she was pushing too hard. Suddenly he was overcome by the need to put some distance between them. "Look, Kelly, the only reason you got involved in the first place was because you wanted a little excitement." He couldn't seem to stop the words, though he knew they weren't true. He was positive that it was more than that for her. He knew what she felt for him. But he couldn't . . . wouldn't allow himself to admit it. "Besides," he said, "there's no such thing as team effort. Everyone is on his own, all alone in life. The sooner you realize that, the better off you'll be."

Silence dragged like a deadweight between them. Why didn't he say what he really felt about her? Why couldn't he let her know how much she now meant in his life?

Kelly stared at Bill, unable to believe what she was hearing. Was this the same man who had held her in his arms yesterday, the man who had spoken so tenderly and lovingly to her?

"You seem so open on the outside," she said. "Smiling blue eyes. But it's all a lie, isn't it? Inside you're locked up, closed, too superior to share yourself with anyone."

His mouth tightened as he recognized the truth in what she was saying. He *was* unable to open up, to love—not because he felt superior but because he felt so terribly afraid. The old refrain played over and over again in his mind. *You're a loser . . . loser . . . loser . . .*

He clenched his jaw to seal the wound. "I don't need to share myself with anyone. I don't need anyone."

Kelly watched him closely, saw the hardening of his jaw, the downward turn of his mouth. He was like a rock—hard, unyielding, hurling himself against any emotional obstacle, shattering it like glass on his way through life. "I wonder how many people you really think you fool," she said quietly, and her eyes captured his in a rare moment of naked truth.

He was the first to look away.

CHAPTER TWELVE

Jake lifted his worn duffelbag to the bed and began rifling through it for the bottle of whiskey that lay tucked between the folds of his underwear. After he found it he unscrewed the cap and poured a hefty swig into the glass that sat on the bathroom counter. He stared for a moment at the dark liquid, toasted some unseen ghost that wandered up from his past, then drank it down in one large gulp.

He poured another shot and moved to the window. He was in the old part of Bangkok's Oriental Hotel, which he preferred to the new section, and he had a perfect view of the pool and terrace and gardens below. Just beyond the hotel grounds was the Chao

Phraya River and, on its opposite bank, the Temple of Dawn. He had been here in this very room only two years before during the Thai bicentennial, when the royal barges carried the king of Thailand and his queen down the River of Kings from the Summer Palace at Bang-Pa-In to the Grand Palace here in Bangkok.

That was one thing Lambert was damn good about; they didn't complain about the expense account. Jake always stayed in the best places wherever he went, ate in the finest restaurants, and enjoyed as many local delights as he could find time for. And Bangkok had some of the best local delights he had ever sampled. In no other country had he ever found women who treated a man better than here.

And not only did he enjoy this particular hotel, but it also happened to be the same one in which the tour group was staying. He wanted to keep close tabs on Bill Clayton. It wasn't enough now just to get the chip back. He wanted to know what Clayton was planning to do with it. He wanted to know exactly what was going on.

Jake slammed the glass of whiskey down on the desk as he stared out the window. Fury and confusion over Watterman's behavior ate with the alcohol into his bloodstream. What was with George anyway! Jake had flown to Frankfurt yesterday at Watterman's command and had to endure the presence of all those other fat-assed executives. But the worst part was the private conversations with George, who was angry, and rightly so, that Clayton had switched chips on him. But Jake wasn't going to take the blame for that.

"Forty-eight hours," George had said. "That's all you've got to get that chip away from Clayton. I don't care how you do it. Just get it."

Forty-eight hours or else what? Jake wondered. George had never laid down ultimatums with him before. What was different this time? Something that Jake couldn't see was pushing Watterman over the edge. He was rapidly losing his grip. But they had been friends for a long time, and Jake was a man who worried about his friends. He would do his best to help him get the chip, but he was also going to get to the bottom of this whole mystery.

Jake watched at the window for a minute longer as young villagers swam in the murky water of the river, diving down into its brown depths, coming back up with a chipped glass in their hands. One would smile triumphantly, pour the sludge from the glass, and hand it to a friend in a small boat nearby. Then, once again, he would dive down into the mud for another treasure.

Jake sat down on the peach-colored couch and propped his feet up on the coffee table. He had to plan his strategy very carefully. Bill Clayton was definitely not a force to be taken lightly. That had been his mistake in the first place, assuming that because the guy was young and American he wouldn't know his butt from a hole in the ground.

As was his habit, Jake began to visualize the events that had taken place as if they were listed chronologically on a piece of paper. Before him was a blank sheet and it was up to him to lay down the pertinent facts, separating the chaff from the crucial grains, laying it out in sequence.

Where had it all begun? What was the first event that had taken place? Was it when Kleinman and Dawson first stole the chip from Lambert Technologies? No, it had to have been the decision to steal it, or perhaps even the development of the chip and its potential use. Obviously there were several parties who wanted or needed it. But why? And who?

Staring off into space at his imaginary piece of paper, Jake began to collate it all. Dawson and Kleinman had helped develop the chip, realized its potential on the open market, found a buyer for it, and then had simply taken it away from Lambert.

They were obviously in a hurry to get it out of Germany because they had given it to their contact as he passed through the Frankfurt airport. But where did Clayton fit in? Sure, he was the pickup, the one who would carry it safely out of the country. But to whom and for what purpose?

There was something about that American that didn't quite fit the puzzle, as if he were as bewildered by all of this as Jake, or as if he were being used in a game of chance. But someone, somewhere, knew the rules and held the strings—Jake had to find him.

In his mind he checked off the first two events that had happened. All right, so then Clayton took the chip to Delhi, where he was to hand it over to Fritz Graber, a small-time fence for a variety of international goods. But before he could give the chip to him, Fritz was whisked out of the picture and found two days later floating facedown in a flooded irrigation ditch.

So Clayton still had the chip. Perhaps he was working on his own now, hoping to find a buyer. Or maybe he was receiving his instructions from someone else. But if he was working for himself, why had he met with George? That was another thing that grated like sandpaper along Jake's spine. George had gone behind his back, met with Clayton, and hadn't even told Jake until yesterday. Who the hell was in charge of this investigation anyway!

One thing was sure now. The time had come to get tough with Bill Clayton. He had hoped that he could retrieve the chip through intimidation. But now he knew it was going to take more than that. Soon it would be time for the final showdown.

Kelly held her camera up to her eye, trying to capture the essence of this beautiful, ancient land. As far as she could see rose the ruins of what was once the capital of Thailand. Ayudhaya's glory as the capital of Siam had lasted from 1350 until 1569, when the Burmese attacked in full force and burned the Buddhist temples to the ground. Only a few remaining statues and crematoria remained. But, blending with the flowers and grass, their presence was still quite imposing.

She moved closer to one of the statues, aiming her camera upward for an elongated shot of a Buddha. After taking several photographs from different angles, Kelly moved on to join the tour. Despite all the signs kindly asking tourists not to climb on the monuments, the Parkers sent their kids scampering up the ancient ruins, posed them in the most darling of all possible poses, and fired away with their camera. Even Muffy was sitting on the lap of one Buddha, holding two fingers as horns behind the statue's head while Damien Brewster took a picture of her. Then, wrapping a possessive arm around her waist, he lifted her down to the ground for a passionate embrace.

Kelly turned away and took a deep breath. Being with these people was proving to be more of a drain as each day passed. Ever since that day in Bombay when Bill told her he needed no one, she had been struggling to keep her spirits up. It was as if she were floating in a kind of limbo, unable to touch anything concrete or solid or real.

She had certainly had her taste of adventure. She couldn't deny that. It was one of the things she had wanted all her life. Something new, different, exciting. She had had it in the palm of her hand. And she had been a participant. Not just a watcher, but a doer. But her need for adventure had led her into Bill Clayton's arms. Too willing, too ready, too vulnerable.

He had said he didn't need her. He didn't need anyone. But she knew that wasn't true. He was afraid to need anyone. If only she knew why. If only he would open up to her.

As the group rode in the bus to the King of

Thailand's Summer Palace, Kelly glanced across at Bill sitting in the aisle seat a few rows ahead of her. His profile was firm, sure, full of unshakable confidence. It was a façade. It had to be! No one could be that sure of their every move. No one could actually like living as an island, apart from the rest of the world, closed off from love and friendship.

Kelly filed off the bus with the rest of the tourists and followed Angel through the grounds of the Summer Palace. He told the tale of one of the ancient Ramas who built a shrine there in memory of his beautiful queen. They had traveled by royal barge to the palace. When the barge pulled into the grounds, all the adoring subjects waited for their ruler and his lovely queen. But the boat that was carrying her capsized and she was tossed into the river. Because of a rigid law that forbade them to touch a royal person, the subjects were forced to watch their beloved queen drown within a few feet of them.

Kelly's eyes shifted to Bill, who was standing only six feet away. He was standing on the bank of the river, peering down into its depths.

She walked over and stood beside him. "Broken into any bedrooms lately?"

He glanced at her with a lopsided grin, then turned back to the river. "Nah. I've got the hots for Edna Blumberg, but she keeps her room locked up tight as a drum."

"Too bad."

"Yeah, it's rough." He smiled at her and shook his head. "Where the hell have you been the last couple of days?"

She shrugged. "Following you around the world."

"If that's not a case of the blind leading the blind, I don't know what is." He pulled her into his arms and smiled down into her face. "I've missed you. I've missed having you in my arms and in my bed."

A light breeze lifted a few strands of hair from his forehead and Kelly reached up with her free fingers to comb it back in place. Peace hung in the fragrant roses around them.

"Is that so?" she whispered, loving the feel of his hands stroking her back.

He kissed the top of her head. "Yeah, honest. I think that as well as the Rama who lost his queen, I probably have a few rules that need some bending."

She looked up at him. "Maybe we've just let the past rule us for too long. I know I have and . . . well, maybe you have too."

There was a long moment of silence, and she wondered if perhaps she'd said too much.

But finally he spoke. "You know, Kelly, you are one perceptive lady."

"Perceptive enough to be included in your plans for the chip?" she goaded him.

He smiled enticingly and ran his fingers through her hair. "That and much much more."

Her breath came out in a swift flow. "When do we start?"

"Tonight."

CHAPTER THIRTEEN

Patpong was not just another street in Bangkok. Like Soi Cowboy and New Petchburi, it was a way of life. A miracle of life, some men might say, offering the most complete massages, the prettiest Thai girls, outrageously priced drinks, and endless noise.

In the dim hours just after dawn, it was narrow and quiet and unassuming. But when the sun went down, it shook off its sleepy cocoon, cranked up the rock and roll and the dazzling lights, and attracted men and women from around the world with its internationally famous delights.

Bill checked the note in his pocket once again for the address as he and Kelly walked down Suriwong Road, turning right onto Pat-pong Two.

"Are you sure this is the place?" she asked, a tinge of incredulity slipping through her voice. Barkers hung in the doorways of bars with names like Sugar Shack, Mike's Place, Roxy, and Pink Panther. "Where are we to meet this man?"

A barker standing in the doorway of a place called Takara called out to Kelly. "Hey, lady, you want massage? We make good massage. You buy?"

Kelly bowed her head, pretending she had not heard him.

Bill cleared his throat and chuckled, wrapping his arm around Kelly's waist. "Foxy Lady."

"Please," she grimaced. "Not you too."

"No, that's where we are meeting Lon Chia."

"Oh," she said, embarrassed. "How did you find out about him anyway?"

"I took all those circuit boards to my office yesterday and I started asking around for the name of someone who had the equipment to analyze computer hardware. A friend of mine gave me Lon Chia's name. Apparently he's the best."

"What did they say about the chip that was

211

missing from their board . . . the one you took out and gave to George?"

"I bought some time by telling them that a new one ʼwas to be sent from the Denver office in a week. The part was defective. I'm just hoping that I'll have it back from Watterman by then and I can send it back here where it belongs."

Bill held Kelly's hand as they passed through a low doorway into the dark interior of the Foxy Lady. Music blared from the large speakers on each side of the bar and the smell of beer and sweat lingered around the empty table where they were seated. Go-go girls pounded their feet and rotated their hips to the rock and roll. A large glass wall separated the main part of the bar from a smaller room where young women sat and watched television, knitted, or read.

"What do you suppose that is?" Kelly asked, pointing to the other room.

Bill leaned close and spoke softly. "Those are the girls for sale."

Kelly looked shocked. "Are you kidding! You mean they just sit there knitting away until some man wants to buy a little of their time?"

Bill nodded. "A different way of life."

"I'll say. And how do you know so much about those girls anyway?"

"Instinct?"

"Right," she murmured, turning her attention to the sounds and sights and smells around them. It had a mesmerizing effect on both of them, on Kelly for the sheer novelty of it all, and on Bill for the elemental sensuality that hung in every molecule of air in the room.

A short man sat down at the table with Bill and Kelly. "You like?" he asked, sweeping his arm to encompass the room. He had gray wisps of hair that stuck straight out all over his head and his face was crinkled with amusement, leaving only tiny slits for eyes. "You are Mr. Clayton?"

"Yes." Bill stretched out his hand in greeting. "Lon Chia?"

The old man nodded and turned to Kelly, extending a hand to her. "And you?"

"I'm Kelly."

"Perfect!" Lon clapped his hands together. "This is the place for you two. You come here. You drink a little, you watch the beautiful ladies, you have a body massage, then you go home and make love. Perfect place for lovers."

Lon Chia spoke fluent English, yet the tonal quality of his Thai language prohibited the pronunciation of certain consonants. But his meaning came through loud and clear.

213

Kelly stared dumbfounded for a long moment at the man before turning a red face toward Bill. He smiled and winked at her and a subtle heat spread through her body at the thought that maybe, just maybe, Lon was right.

"Did all of this start during the Vietnam War?" Bill asked.

"Patpong did not come into existence until after the end of the war. There were other streets during the sixties and early seventies that were very popular with the soldiers. Petchburi Road, for example. But they are not much now. This is the center of the action. A man name Pat Pong owns this street and Patpong One also. If you want to have a business here, you must rent the property from Pat Pong. Very shrewd idea, no?"

Bill agreed. "For as long as it lasts anyway."

At that moment a woman came over and whispered something into Lon's ear. He turned back to Bill and Kelly and shrugged apologetically.

"I am so sorry. But it is time for my massage." He smiled at the surprised look on their faces. "Yes, you must try a Thai massage. So relaxing." He grinned at Bill. "Not at all like you Americans have. Not like YMCA," he giggled. "No, no. I must go."

"But what about the chip?" Bill asked.

"Oh, yes. We will meet again. You will meet me for dinner at Nick's Number One."

"Tonight?"

"Yes. At eleven o'clock."

"Where is Nick's . . . ?"

"Nick's Number One. Not far from here. You will take a taxi there. Driver will know where to go." Lon stood to go. "You will meet me there?"

"Yes," Bill nodded. "We'll see you then." They watched Lon walk away, his stride springy with anticipation of the nightly ritual.

After he was gone, Bill ordered drinks for both of them and they watched as one girl after another was chosen from the glass-enclosed room. Bill leaned toward Kelly and whispered close to her ear, "What do you think about what Lon said? About the massages?"

Kelly rested her elbows on the table, cupping her chin in her palm. "Sounds . . . interesting."

"I am a great masseur," he smiled.

"Is that so?"

"And I'm very very cheap."

"Now you're talking." She laughed lightly, aware of every movement of Bill's fingers as they slid up her arm, brushing the side of her breast. His hand began kneading her shoulder, lifting into her hair to press the tips of his

215

fingers into her scalp. "When do we . . . when are we . . ." Her breath was shallow and rapid.

"Tonight," he whispered. "I promise you the most complete massage you've ever had in your life. Tonight."

The taxi stopped in front of a big white house almost hidden with overgrown brush. Bill and Kelly stepped out of the car and climbed the steps to the front porch. Inside, the entryway was dark and mysterious. The walls were papered with miscellaneous business cards at least two inches deep, creating a textured look in the dark.

"Welcome." A large balding man with thick lips and a huge smile greeted them. "I am Nick. Welcome to my restaurant."

Bill nodded. "We're looking for a friend. Lon Chia."

"Ha-ha!" he cried. "Wonderful. Come this way, please."

Nick led them into another room filled with old, rough wooden tables. The lighting in the restaurant was provided by candlelight alone. They were seated at a table with Lon and a beautiful young Thai woman.

"Your guests have arrived," said Nick. "Welcome one and all." He seated Kelly and Bill, then slipped into the shadows to oversee the preparation of their meal.

"Everyone is so friendly here," Kelly marveled.

"But of course," Lon laughed. "Thailand is the Land of Smiles. This is Chin Lee," he said, introducing the lady next to him. "She does not speak your language."

"Hello," Bill and Kelly greeted her, and the young woman pressed her hands together and bowed slightly.

"Chin Lee is my masseuse." At their startled expressions, Lon giggled.

Kelly smiled self-consciously at the woman, then opened the menu in front of her. Seeking to get Lon Chia off of what seemed to be his favorite subject, she asked if he'd ever been to America.

"Oh, yes," he answered. "I received my undergraduate degree in engineering from M.I.T., took an MBA at Stanford, then went into law at Harvard."

"What do you do here in Bangkok?" Bill asked.

"I run a small computer shop . . . and I live." He smiled enigmatically. "We are not an ambitious people," he explained. "Not like you Americans or the Japanese. We prefer to enjoy the simpler things in life." He patted Chin Lee's hand. "A good massage, potent drinks, a plate of beef satay and steamed vegetables. To us, those are the things to be valued most in life."

He looked back and forth between Kelly and Bill. "You are both young, so young. I believe you have a saying in your country—stop and smell the roses. That is a good saying. Very true, very true. Slow down and enjoy each other."

Bill reached under the table for Kelly's hand and squeezed it tightly. "You're a wise man, Mr. Chia."

"No," he shrugged. "Just old. Now"—he sat up straight and clasped his hands on the table, all business and efficiency—"what is this microchip you wish me to see."

Bill reached into his pocket, but pulled his fingers back out without the chip. His reluctance was evident in his eyes. "Lon, you have to understand something. In the last few days I've been tailed by some gangster named Jake, I've had several people double-cross me. I've had to learn not to . . ."

"Not to trust," Lon nodded. "Yes, I can understand that. It is the same with me. I believe in everyone, but I trust no one."

Silence hung heavy for several seconds between the two men.

"So," Lon mused. "You are not sure you can trust me with this marvelous chip. Am I right?"

Bill nodded.

"Ron Miller told you to come to me, did he not?"

"Yes. He said he had worked with you many times."

"Ron is a good man. I have never lied to him, never cheated him. I won't say I have never cheated anyone, but . . ." Lon shrugged noncommittally. "But I have never cheated my friends or the friends of my friends."

Bill nodded with some inner resolution and reached into his pocket for the plastic bag that held the chip. "I just want to know what this really is," he said as he handed it to Lon.

Lon nodded. "Well, we will learn all of this tomorrow. You will come see me at my store. Here is my card." He reached into his jacket and handed Bill a business card. "I am just off Ploenchit Road on Rajadamri. You will come to my store at ten o'clock. I will have the answers for you."

"Thank you, Lon. It will be such a relief." Bill glanced at Kelly. "For both of us."

"Now"—the hands moved off the table and the professional look was gone from Lon's face. He smiled at Chin Lee and picked up a menu—"we will order. You must try Nick's Kobe beef. It is the best in Bangkok."

Jake sat across the street from Nick's in a

small, dirty bar, sipping a lukewarm beer and eating soggy fish. He was waiting. He knew they had to come out sooner or later. So he would simply bide his time.

At a quarter to one they emerged from the restaurant. There were four of them; Clayton, the girl, an old guy, and some local talent. But, damn it, they were splitting up, going in different directions. Well, Clayton and the girl were staying at his hotel; he would be able to find them later on if the old man proved to be a dry run. But he had to follow him. Otherwise he might never find him again. He had to see if the old man now had the chip.

Downing the last swig of beer, Jake dropped fifty baht onto the table and walked down the street, following Lon Chia on his circuitous route to his home above the computer shop.

Jake waited until Lon entered the store, but only a second before the door closed wedged his foot into the slim opening. Lon Chia turned, surprised, as Jake flung the door wide and stepped into the shop, now illuminated only by the lights from the street that shone through the window.

The two men didn't speak for a long moment, but only stared at each other, Lon wary and Jake threatening. Finally the older man spoke. "What is it that you want?"

"The chip."

"What chip?"

"Don't be stupid, old man. I don't want to hurt you."

"I always try not to be stupid. I do not wish to be hurt."

"Then give me the chip."

"What chip?"

Jake's eyes narrowed to tiny slits, ominous and black. "I'm sorry you said that." Like the strike of a cobra, Jake's arm shot out, catching Lon on the lower left jaw. The old man stumbled backward and Jake knew he had him now. He moved forward decisively.

He got the surprise of his life.

Lon ducked down, dodging the next blow by inches. But when he came back up it was behind the power of his fist in Jake's stomach. This time Jake stumbled backward, staring with stunned awe at the old man.

Lon wiped a rivulet of sweat from his temple. "Yes, you are surprised. In this country we learn to fight at a very young age. So come, show me what you can do against my Thai boxing."

Jake's deep breath sounded more like a growl as he lunged once more for the little man who dared to show such foolhardy courage in front of him, but before three minutes had passed, he was flat on his back amidst overturned tables, scattered electronic equipment, and a shattered lamp.

"You had enough, Mr. Karate Expert?" Lon laughed, but pain was evident in the strained sound. He was leaning against the wall, forcing the pain to stay down until he had finished with this strange dark man. "Enough?"

Jake sat on the floor, his arm up and his fingers clutching the edge of the counter. He hurt. He hurt bad. But a flame of anger and energy surged through him, forcing him up and out toward his waiting opponent.

The crack of a rib was the next sound to rent the air of the small computer shop just off Ploenchit Road in the Land of Smiles.

Rather than take a taxi, Bill and Kelly rode back to the hotel in a samlor, a type of motorized rickshaw, better known as a tuk-tuk. The driver wound slowly through the narrow streets of Bangkok, slicing through the clear, warm night. Bill slipped his arm around Kelly's back and her head dropped onto his shoulder.

"So what's it worth to you?"

"What's that?" she asked, pivoting her head on his shoulder to look at him.

"The massage."

"I don't know what qualifications you

have," she said with a superior lilt. "Do you come with references?"

"Many."

Her face grew serious. "That's what I was afraid of."

He pulled her tighter against him. "Hey, who cares. It shouldn't matter. I mean if it really bothers you or if you want to talk about it, we can."

She turned back to him and lifted her fingers to the top button of his shirt. "I don't really want to know . . . I guess."

Bill tilted her head back and covered her lips with his own. The soft night billowed around them. "We're two people, together, wanting each other. Maybe we shouldn't ask for or expect more."

Kelly smiled up at Bill. "Oh, but I expect a lot for my money."

He groaned softly and nuzzled her neck. "Sounds like my kind of challenge."

The tuk-tuk pulled up in front of the Oriental and Kelly and Bill stepped out and paid the driver. Their rooms were in the same end of the hallway, but they didn't stop at hers. Instead, they went directly to his.

Once inside, Bill tossed his key on the desk and leaned against the door, watching Kelly as she stood self-consciously in the middle of the room.

223

"So," she said, looking everywhere but at Bill. "Do we . . . do you want . . . ?" She sighed and forged ahead. "Is this massage supposed to be with or without my clothes?"

Bill cocked his head and grinned at her. He pushed away from the door and stepped up to her. His fingers slowly unfastened the top button of her blouse, his eyes looking directly into hers. "What a foolish question," he whispered, lowering his mouth to her neck.

"Yes," she sighed. "I guess it was." She stood very still and let him undress her and lower her to the bed. She watched him as he slowly removed his own clothes, dropping them on top of hers on the floor.

He sat on the bed beside her and began his magic. His fingers moved like a snail down her spine, sliding, pressing, rotating. His hand worked on the back of her neck, her shoulders, kneading the flesh down her arms until her body was a lump of warm clay in his hands, pliable enough for him to mold into any shape.

"Where have you been all my life?" she moaned, replete with the exquisite pleasure.

His response was to lovingly bring his lips to the top of her spine, moving inch by inch down each vertebra. After her back had been worshipped by his fingers and mouth, he slowly moved to her legs, massaging her thighs and calves with the same deliberate sensuality.

She couldn't have moved a muscle if she had wanted to. She was warm and loose and totally his.

"Now," he commanded with his mouth against the back of her neck. "Turn over. I'm only half finished."

Once she was on her back she waited breathlessly for him to begin again. His hands were everywhere, stroking, searching, finding, and subduing. Her breath was a shallow whisper of anxious need as she moved her own hands down the sides of his hips and around to the tops of his thighs. Her fingers wrapped tightly around him, impetuous and inciting. A sweet agony seemed to tear him in two. His mouth moved over her, tasting, praising, every slope and valley on her body. And the soft moans that came from her lips pushed him further, harder, wanting to unleash the same ungovernable hunger in her that was in him.

Her fingers clutched his hair while the passion swirled through her bloodstream, carrying her to a height she had never reached before.

When he finally moved inside of her, she felt all energy in the universe concentrated in that one union, in the pulsating electrical force that was generated between their two bodies. The burning need she felt for this man's possession consumed her totally. Even in love, Bill was a driven man. He was compelled to possess, to control, to dominate her. And she gave herself up completely to his power. It was what she had waited for all her life. And it was all she had dreamed and feared it would be.

CHAPTER FOURTEEN

Jake pulled the door handle on the taxi several times before he could make the door open. He stepped gingerly onto the pavement in front of the Oriental Hotel, but even the slightest bit of weight on his feet pressed the pain upward through his body. Stiff and bruised, he staggered into the hotel, ignoring the curious stares of the doorman who was on duty at this still-dark hour of morning.

Jake tried to keep from groaning out loud as he crossed the marble lobby, staying clear of the bright green rug as he moved to the elevator. He was getting too old for this. Maybe he should retire. Maybe George was right. He couldn't handle it anymore. Someone else should take over. Too old. He reached into his pocket. Damn! Even his cigars were crushed.

As soon as he was locked in his room, he let the groan finally escape and collapsed onto his bed, falling unconscious almost immediately.

Kelly stirred, but didn't wake up. She nestled back into the curve of Bill's arm and settled herself to sleep. He watched her. The morning light filtered through the space between the curtains, and he was able to watch her in her peaceful repose.

As he had been for over a week, he was consumed by her. The way she curled her body to fit the contours of his, her breath soft and peaceful in the early morning, her fingers resting lightly just above his hipbone, her ash brown hair strewn across his chest.

I don't really need you. I don't need anyone! He looked up at the ceiling, but immediately his eyes were drawn back to her. She moved again and her thigh rose to drape over his. She didn't know what he was like, what his whole life was about. She didn't know anything about him. And who was she anyway? Just another woman.

His hand touched her hair and he fingered a long strand while he thought about his relationships with other women. What was it about Kelly that made him want to reach over and enclose her, pull her against him, force his way inside of her and somehow wrench himself away from this hold she had on him?

Kelly shifted and opened her eyes. Tilting her head back, she looked up at Bill and smiled. He groaned, lost in the gray of her eyes, and sank down deeper into the warm moist depths of her body, her mind, and her entire being.

It was true that Lon Chia's store was on Rajadamri, just off Ploenchit, but Bill and Kelly had to walk up and down the street several times before they actually found the shop. It was small and nestled back a bit from the street. Only Chia's name hung on an insignificant sign in the front window.

After several knocks Lon finally opened the locked door. "What on earth happened to you?" Kelly cried.

His face on one side was swollen to twice its normal size and his upper lip sported a deep red slit. But he tried to smile and wave off their worry as he invited them into his ransacked shop. "It was a slight diversion from my usual night, nothing more. I would imagine your Mr. Jake is in worse shape than I am in this morning."

"Jake?"

"Yes. I assume him to be the same man who has been following you. He must have seen you give me the chip."

Bill's mouth was tight. "Did he get it?"

"The chip? Oh, my, no. I told you that I could be trusted with it. Lon Chia never makes a promise that he cannot keep." He stooped and picked up the pieces of a broken bottle and tossed them into the trash can behind the counter. "However, this game is certainly causing a stir."

Bill frowned. "Hardly what I would call a game," he mumbled.

Following Lon's signal, he and Kelly walked through a curtain into the back of the shop. Parts of computers, disk drives, printers, circuit boards, video display units, and a thousand other tiny bits of computer hardware filled the room. There was hardly even space to walk, but they trailed Lon over to a table in the center of the room.

He sat in a hard-backed chair in front of a computer with Bill and Kelly standing behind him. "We've been through so much," Kelly sighed. "It will be a relief to at least know why."

"Why, indeed," Lon shrugged. "You have been through much for a game."

Bill frowned again. "It's been a little more serious than that."

Lon turned around in his chair and looked at him. His gaze shifted to Kelly briefly before returning to Bill. "No, that is not what I mean. I mean this component is a game chip."

Kelly glanced at Bill, but he wasn't moving. His expression was totally blank. His eyes registered the surprise first. They narrowed on the old man before shifting to Kelly. "A game?"

Lon nodded and shrugged. "I'm afraid so."

Bill shoved his hands into the pockets of his jeans. "That's impossible. You've made a mistake. You've got the wrong chip."

"This is the chip you gave me," Lon insisted. "Look." He turned back around to his keyboard and video terminal. "First I put it through some simulations, ran a program that tried different combinations of inputs to read the outputs, just to see what this thing was doing, you see.

"I eliminated all sorts of possibilities this way. The only thing left was that it was some sort of video display generator. Then, of course, I had to hook it up to my terminal, and what did I see?"

Bill and Kelly waited silently while Lon flipped on the machine and typed in the appropriate commands for the computer to translate. Wavy lines appeared first on the screen, dissolving slowly into a three-dimensional grid. "You see?"

"No," they both answered in unison.

Lon sighed and stood up. He set the video terminal aside, pried loose the top of the computer's memory case, and slipped in another circuit board. Closing the lid, he pushed a program diskette into the drive, and typed in some new instructions.

What appeared next on the screen were the dotted outlines of spaceships and fat little monsters.

"I know that game," Kelly cried, missing the disgusted look Bill sent her way. "Space Wars. But . . . I don't know, it looks so different, so . . ."

"Dimensional," Lon beamed.

Bill stared at the little man. "Three dimensional? Is that what you're saying, that this is some sort of chip for three-dimensional display games?"

"That is indeed what I am saying."

"I have been chased across two continents for a goddamn game chip for morons who play arcade games!"

"Morons?" Kelly snapped, planting her hands on her waist.

"That's right, morons. Don't you even realize what has happened, Kelly? We have been chased by men who obviously intend to kill for a game."

"Yes, Mr. Bill," Lon smiled. "But you obviously have no idea what something like this could mean on the open market. There is nothing like this out there, and the first one who develops three-D for games will make a fortune. An absolute fortune. It will revolutionize the entire game industry, even the entire computer industry. It is the way of the future." Lon pointed to the game on the video display. "This, my American friends, is the future. It is upon us."

"Why would no one say that? Why didn't George and all the others who have been tailing us say what it was?"

Lon shrugged. "Perhaps they did not know or did not want you to know."

"But they had to know, at least George Watterman did. It was his chip!"

"That is a puzzle, I agree. Perhaps this Mr. George is . . . how do you say, pulling a number on everyone?"

Bill thought for a moment. "We know he's up to something. The question is what. If he were doing this as a secret move to make money for the company, it seems he would have had a key person, someone he trusted, negotiating with us. If it's not a secret, why wouldn't he have sicced Interpol on us? After all, we have supposedly committed a crime. They think we stole the chip from the company."

"Perhaps he is doing it for some sort of personal gain," Lon suggested.

Bill nodded slowly, sorting through the details. "Could be."

Kelly turned to Bill. "It is possible, isn't it?"

He looked at her for a long moment, thinking of the incidents that brought them together and of how far they had come in such a few short days. He shook his head. "At this point, anything is possible."

Sunken eyes stared back at Jake from the skull-like face. As much of a wimp as Jimmy Graves was, it always gave Jake the creeps to look at him. They were standing in the bathroom of Bangkok's airport, Graves pressed against the row of sinks.

"So why did you back off?" Jake demanded.

Graves shrugged his bony shoulders. "I'd think you'd know the answer to that yourself, Balletoni."

Jake shoved him back harder against the edge of the sink, his hand grasping Graves's collar. "If I knew the answers, why the hell would I be here in the cesspool with you?"

Graves twisted his head to straighten the collar of his shirt. "We found out the artificial intelligence chip wasn't the one that was stolen from Lambert's lab."

Jake frowned. "What do you mean, wasn't the one? There's only one."

"Nope." Graves shook his head, taking great pleasure in the fact that he knew more about this than Jake Balletoni did. "There are two. The AI chip that Randall-Impex was highly interested in obtaining by any means necessary." He grinned self-confidently. "Which is why yours truly posed as a government official." He cleared his throat when he noticed Jake's jaw growing tighter. "And then there was the chip that was actually stolen."

"What is it?"

"Don't know. Maybe you ought to ask Watterman that. He seems to be the only one with a full deck of cards in this game. Whatever it is, he sure seems to think it's worth a lot of trouble. Anyway, Randall-Impex is no longer interested, so I'm flying home. Case closed."

Jake stared at Jimmy Graves until the other man realized he wasn't even looking at him. Graves slipped quietly out of the bathroom, leaving Jake to stare into a space of air filled with a dozen unanswered questions.

The case wasn't closed for him. It was just opening up.

235

CHAPTER FIFTEEN

If Kelly saw one more Buddha, she was going to scream. Gold Buddhas, emerald Buddhas, black Buddhas, bronze Buddhas, reclining, sitting, standing, kneeling . . . It was almost enough to make a person swear off religion forever. The tour group had been walking for what seemed like hours inside the grounds of the Grand Palace. Gold and precious gems decorated the buildings, which were adorned with ornate spires and carved statues and minarets. It was almost gaudy in its splendor, giving her the feeling that she had entered a Hollywood set that was made, not really of gold and marble, but of Styrofoam and fiberboard.

While the three widows from Iowa were ooohing and aaahing at appropriate intervals, the Parker tykes sat astride a couple of huge gargoyles outside one of the buildings yelling "Giddiyap," and the Caldwells again lugged a half dozen shopping bags loaded with souvenirs.

Bill was deep in conversation with a young Thai student who was trying to sell him some of his artwork, so Kelly decided to move on ahead and get some pictures of the various group members for her article.

She lifted her camera, zooming in on Muffy and Angel. His forehead was creased in a thousand tiny lines as he tried to make sense of something she was saying to him. Her arcane vocabulary had been a puzzle to him since they began the trip, and right now he couldn't make head or tail of what she was mumbling about. Kelly smiled. It would be a great photograph.

She adjusted the focus and laid her finger over the shutter. But before she could press the button, the camera was wrenched from her hands and it fell to the ground, landing directly on the lens.

Kelly's arm was caught in a steel grip and yanked behind her back painfully. Another arm wrapped around her shoulders from behind and the large hand loosely clutched a revolver. It was only seconds before she saw his face, but the painful surprise seemed to last forever.

"Mr.—Mr. Watterman!" she gasped as he pulled her behind the building, leading her away from the rest of the group. "What are you . . ."

He didn't answer, but kept leading her toward the street. She tried to turn around to signal Bill or one of the others, but he held her too tightly to do anything but move forward.

"Your boyfriend did a real stupid thing."

She thought of screaming but, as if her intentions translated to him through her fear, he jammed the gun in her side as they walked.

"That wasn't smart, giving me the wrong chip," he growled against her ear.

"It was a . . . mistake. He was planning to—"

"Shut up!" He pushed her toward a waiting taxi and shoved her into the backseat. He followed and closed the door.

The driver turned around and saw the look of panic on the woman's face. "Help me!" she cried, but George stifled any intervention by pointing the gun directly at the driver's head.

"Turn around, drive to the airport, and don't let me hear a sound out of you."

The airport! Kelly's mind was screaming the word over and over again. The airport! He

238

was taking her somewhere. Away from Bill, away from all the others. "Where are we going?" she whispered.

George leaned back against the seat and directed the gun at her head. Slowly, deliberately, maliciously, he lowered the gun by inches. Over eyes, down her nose, onto her mouth, dropping over her chin, sliding lazily down her chest and stomach, then rising and stopping at the level of her heart.

"We're going on a little trip, you and I." His smile was smug, but there was an anxious tic in one eye that spelled only one thing. Fear. He was as scared as she was.

She knew it was probably false hope, but she grabbed at that tiny gesture, like a drowning victim clutching a cluster of seaweed, in the irrational belief that it might pull her to safety. She looked down at her hands in her lap to avoid staring at him. But she knew the gun hadn't moved from her chest. They were going on a little trip.

Bill paid the boy forty-five baht for a couple of pictures of sampans, much more than they were probably worth, but they were nicely done. Maybe Kelly would want one of them. He walked over toward Angel, who was now signaling everyone that it was time to head back to the bus.

He scanned the area for Kelly, hoping she hadn't forgotten what time the bus was supposed to leave to go back to the hotel. He checked the group now standing around the guide. Everyone was here. The Caldwells, whose arms seemed at least six inches longer than when they started on the trip; Mr. Fowler, grumbling about the inadequacies of one or another ethnic group; the Parkers, cramming huge suckers into their kids' mouths to keep them happy; Muffy, bored and sardonic as usual, and again without her aunt, who was snoring away on the bus; Damien Brewster, looking hot and miserable in his too tight slacks; the three widows, hyperventilating over the landscaping of the palace grounds; Professor Evanston, flicking a limp wrist and gawking at the surroundings with alien wonder; and Angel, clucking like a mother hen as he swept in his brood with a broad wing. They were all there: all except Kelly.

"Miss Kelly where?" Angel asked in his typical manner.

"I don't know." Bill tried to laugh to loosen a strange knot of foreboding that was tightening in his chest. "She's probably taking pictures and just forgot the time."

"But de bus, de bus. It waiting."

"I know that," Bill snapped. "Listen, get

240

everybody else on the bus and I'll find her. We'll be there in just a minute."

Angel's eyes darted about in agitation. All it took for him to go into apoplexy was for the bus to leave five minutes past schedule. "Okee, we wait."

Bill left the group behind him as he went in search of Kelly. He looked everywhere, in every temple where the public was allowed, on every stairway, in each alcove. His heart was beating to an anxious rhythm, knowing instinctively that all was not right, but not yet ready to admit it as a positive fact. She could have gone to a restroom, could be talking to someone, examining some intricate carving, photographing a . . .

He stopped and stared at a couple of boys, their eyes bright and covetous, fingering and ogling a thirty-five millimeter camera. The red and gold striped strap dangled between them, the colors glaring in the noonday sun.

He rushed toward them, shoving them aside and reaching for the camera. "What are you doing? Where did you get this?"

The two boys jumped back, guilty consciences frightening them into silence. Bill knew they probably didn't speak English, but a helpless fear made him hurl his rage at them. He grabbed one of them by the back of

241

the neck. "I asked you where you found this? Where is the woman it belongs to?"

The boy shook his head, his mouth moving silently. "Here," he croaked, surprising Bill enough that he let go of the boy's neck.

"You speak English?"

The boy's shoulders rose in an unconscious show of pride. "Little," he asserted.

"You found this camera here?"

"Yes."

"Where is the lady, the woman it belongs to?"

"No lady." He pointed to the camera. "This, here."

"You didn't see anything happen to the lady? You didn't see where she went?"

"No lady," he repeated.

Bill clenched the camera between his hands and his eyes and jaw clamped shut. Where in hell was she!

He searched the grounds for another half hour, telling himself that she was all right, trying to convince himself that she wasn't hurt or lost or—he couldn't even allow himself to imagine anything more. Why had he let her out of his sight!

He finally went back to the bus to tell the others that he could not find her and to explain how he did find the camera. Angel's

242

concern was tinted with worry over what this might do to his career.

Bill shook his head and closed his eyes. He had to think. She couldn't be far away. But where, damn it, where?

"She must be lost," Angel concluded. "But she will come to hotel. I know it."

Bill glared at the unfortunate guide. "Yeah? And what makes you so damn sure?" he growled. He climbed down out of the bus. "You can all go back to the hotel if you want. I'm waiting here."

He walked back through the palace gate, heading for the spot where the boys had found her camera. She had to be here someplace. He would find her. He had to.

Jake stepped off the elevator just as the tour group was coming back in the door. He started to duck back into it, but he noticed that Bill and Kelly were not with the others. Various group members were noticeably agitated, so he moved in closer to see what he could find out.

"That's what happens when you come to one of these third-world nations," Fowler declared. "You're lucky if you get out of them alive. It's that lawless mentality, I tell you. Primitive, animalistic criminals, that's all these people are."

Edna Blumberg tittered with her two friends. "What if she were taken by some . . . some slave trader or something?"

"Oh, my." Pearl Henshaw fanned herself with a postcard of the Emerald Buddha.

"What a pity." Henry Caldwell shook his head gravely, casting a furtive glance at his wife.

She patted his arm gently. "She'll be found. I'm just sure of it." But her eyes flitted to Henry's with something less than genuine concern.

The desk clerk called to Angel. "Is a Mr. Clayton with you, Mr. Angelique?"

"No, I 'fraid not. He is waiting for one of our tour members who seem to be lost at de moment."

"Well, he received a message a few minutes ago, so I just thought I would give it to him."

"From a woman?" Angel asked.

"No, a man."

"Ah, well." Angel shrugged with uninteres and walked with the others to the elevators

Jake hung back, waiting until all were head ing up to their rooms before he stepped for ward to the desk. He signaled a desk clerk who had been busy when the other clerk spoke to the guide a minute before, and had not heard the exchange. "I'm Bill Clayton. Do you have a message for me?"

"Your room number, please?"

"Six twelve."

"May I see your key, please?"

"I don't have it with me." Jake's mind spun through a thousand excuses.

"I'm sorry then, sir. I cannot—"

"I dropped the key off here before I left this afternoon," he said, trying to remain calmer than he felt.

"One moment, I will check." He watched the clerk pick up the note and two sets of keys from beneath it. Jake sighed with relief. *Good boy, Clayton. I'm sure as hell glad you did that.*

"Here you go, sir."

Jake took the note and moved away from the desk before the other clerk saw him. He didn't know if any of them knew Clayton or not, but he didn't want to take that chance. Walking through the main lobby, he followed the hallway that led to the original section of the hotel and the famous Author's Lounge. He sat down in a white wicker chair and opened the note.

Bill—

Kelly sends her love. She's having a wonderful time in Hong Kong at the Regent and is looking forward to your arrival. I,

245

too, look forward to seeing you and expect that you will bear wonderful gifts as always. If we're not in our room when you get here, leave package at the desk. Kelly will very much appreciate it.

Best regards,
George.

Jake sat back in the chair and stared at the note in his hands. *That goddamn son of a bitch. He's been using me, making me an accomplice in something I know nothing about.* This was kidnapping. And George hadn't even told him what was going on with the damn chip! If there was one thing Jake Balletoni couldn't tolerate, it was being used.

Through this whole charade George had been stepping on Jake's toes, and he damn sure wasn't going to sit back any longer and let it happen without knowing why. Besides that, the man was totally out of control. If Jake didn't stop him now, George might end up doing something really stupid. He would have to save him again as he had so many times before. Only this time he would be saving George from himself.

Bill stood back in the shadows and watched Jake walk out of the airline ticket office. He had been following him since he left the hotel an hour earlier. Bill had waited and searched the palace grounds for almost three hours before he gave up hope of finding her there. Now his only chance was to follow Jake. It might be a long shot, but it was the only shot he had.

He tailed him to the ticket office about five blocks from the hotel, then ducked into a narrow alley between the building Jake entered and the one next to it. He hid behind a pile of discarded cardboard boxes.

About twenty minutes later Jake came out and headed back down the street. Bill grabbed a rock on the ground next to him and tossed it out at Jake's feet.

At the sound of stone against concrete, Jake stopped. He looked down at the rock at his feet, then scanned the area to his left for signs of anyone who might have thrown it. He saw nothing. Cautiously he stepped into the alley, tiny lines fanning out from his narrowed eyes. He detected a movement behind the pile of boxes, but before he could react, a hard body smashed into his ribs.

The pain tore through the wrapping around his already cracked ribs, and sent him spiraling backward. A fist rammed into his jaw before he could dodge the blow. By now the pain had become a numb ache and the will to survive took over.

He jammed his fist into his opponent's stomach, knocking him backward. Only then did he realize whom he was fighting.

Like a charging bull, Bill was on him again and the sounds of bone against bone, accompanied by frequent groans, rent the evening air. They repeatedly knocked each other to the ground, then pulled themselves back up to do battle once more.

After several minutes they both lay on the ground, six feet apart, too exhausted to continue the fight. Bill made one last-ditch effort, drawing himself up and staggering over to Jake. He reached down and pulled the older man to his feet and pushed him into the wall behind him, his forearm blocking his windpipe. "Where the hell is she!" He pressed harder on Jake's throat. "Where is she, damn it!"

Jake's arm flailed about until he was able to reach into his pocket and extract the note that had been left for Bill at the hotel. He waved it in front of him until Bill loosened his hold, letting Jake drop back down to the ground.

He unfolded the sheet of paper and scanned the note that George had dictated over the phone to the desk clerk. His jaw tightened with each word he read. "Go damn it!" He kicked at a loose piece of garbage and sent it skimming past Jake's head, missing him by only a fraction of an inch.

Bill placed his foot on Jake's calf and pressed down hard. "What is your part in this? What do you have to do with George Watterman?"

Jake grimaced with pain as the foot increased its pressure on his leg. He thought about reaching out to trip Clayton, but finally thought better of it. At this point he wasn't even sure Clayton was the one he should be fighting. "Ah, hell," he groaned. "I'm too old for all of this. Let me up and we'll talk about it."

Bill's breath was still ragged and heaving, and his knuckles and jaw hurt like hell, but he wasn't about to let Jake up. "Tell me about Watterman first."

"I work for Lambert," Jake croaked. "Head of security. Damn it, would you get the hell off my leg!"

Bill lightened some of the weight, but didn't yet remove his foot. "Go on."

"George sent me over to Frankfurt to find out what happened to a computer chip, some top-secret project that he'd been working on for a year."

"Who in the company knew what the chip was to be used for?"

"I don't really know. God, that hurts!"

Bill finally removed his foot from Jake's leg and the older man started to stand.

"Stay where you are," Bill commanded.

Jake flopped back down, too weary to argue. "Apparently there were two chips all along," he sighed. "One was an artificial intelligence chip. Some of the key people in the company knew about it and that was what was supposedly stolen. But I found out yesterday that it was another chip that was stolen, one that no one but the scientists who developed it and . . . and George knew about."

"It's a game chip."

"What?" Jake looked at him as if he hadn't heard him correctly.

"I said it's a game chip. Three-dimensional display."

"For those . . . those—"

"Arcade games."

"You're kidding."

"Not in the least. Are you telling me you didn't know?"

Jake leaned his head back against the wall of the building and closed his eyes. He had been beaten to a pulp twice in the last two days for a goddamn game! "No, I didn't know."

"Looks like Watterman is trying to develop

something for his own personal gain," Bill reflected.

Jake opened his eyes and stared at him. As much as he hated to admit it, Bill made sense. And it hit him solidly for the first time that George was probably doing something illegal. He had been too uptight over this one for it to be a company matter. And he had moved in on Jake's territory. Now he had the Milburn girl as hostage. And through it all, through the whole goddamn scam, Jake had been used!

Jake had trusted George, believed in him. They had been friends for so long, gone through so much together. And now, in the end, George had turned against him. That wasn't George! That wasn't the way he operated. Something had driven him to this point of deception and Jake wanted to find out what it was. Despite all his anger and confusion, he was worried. They had been friends for too long.

"You really didn't know, did you?" Bill asked, watching the series of emotions that clouded Jake's expression.

He shook his head slowly, feeling every bit his age. "No, I really didn't know."

Bill reached out a hand and helped Jake to his feet. But his fingers clamped hard around the older man's arm. "You're going to help me find Watterman. We're going to find him —together."

Jake's startled eyes locked with Bill's. Work together! He'd never worked together with anyone in his life. He stared at the cold, hard glare of Clayton's blue eyes and decided not to make any rash decisions just yet. "I gotta have a smoke," he said. He patted his pockets until he came up with a bent cigar. Jamming it into his mouth, he found a match and struck it against the wall, lighting the end of the cigar until the smoke billowed about his head.

It gave him the break he needed. "I work alone," he said, sending a cloud of yellow smoke in Bill's direction.

Bill was undaunted. He leaned toward Jake and his eyes never wavered. "Listen to me you son of a bitch, and listen good. I don't like the way you've been following me for two weeks. I don't like the way you tore into Kelly Milburn's room. I don't like the way you look. I don't like your cigars; and I don't like you. But if you don't help me get to Kelly, and i anything, and I mean anything, has happened to her, I'm coming after you. And I don't care how far I have to track you down, I'm going to catch up with you."

Jake puffed on his cigar, showing no emotion whatsoever. But inside, something told him it was time to back down. Looking into

Bill Clayton's angry eyes, he realized he'd definitely been on the wrong side this time. And there was a hell of a lot of cleaning up to do. Besides, helping Clayton might be the only way he could help George Watterman. He clamped the cigar between his teeth and said, "The next flight for Hong Kong leaves at eight o'clock tonight."

CHAPTER SIXTEEN

Kelly stared with distaste at the breakfast George put in front of her. "I'm not hungry."

"Suit yourself," he mumbled, sitting down before his own plate. "But let it not be said that I tried to starve you."

Kelly glared at her captor for a hostile minute, then looked down at her food. She pushed it away.

The Regent Hotel was a mammoth affair, jutting out from a point on Kowloon and looming over the harbor. Their room on the tenth floor had a wide window looking out on the bay and Hong Kong island beyond. Kelly had spent the hours since early morning doing nothing but watching the barges and ferries glide back and forth from the island to the China mainland, bright sails in the morning sun that gave her something to focus on, something other than why she was here to think about.

She thought about what she had said to Ruth when her editor decided to send her on this tour. "Nothing exciting ever happens on these things," she had said. God, how childish and stupid that sounded to her ears now! What was it she had been looking for all her life? Was it this? Surely not. All she had ever really wanted was someone to show her that she was not the same person as her mother, that life did hold something other than mediocrity for her. Well, she had found that all right. This was about as far from mediocrity as one could get.

And Bill. When she thought of all the preconceived notions she'd had about him when they first met. Because he was so handsome she had simply assumed he'd be an egotistical, arrogant creep. And then, after she got to know him, his need to dominate and control had scared her to death.

She had been so wrong about him. She knew that now. She still didn't understand all the things that drove him so hard, that angered him so easily, that clouded his blue eyes with a veil of secrecy. But that would come in time. For now, it was enough to know that she loved him, and that he loved her.

She looked back at George, happily eating every bite of food on his plate. "You won't get away with this, you know."

George continued chewing while he watched her. She was wearing a peach blouse and blue jeans, her feet were bare, and her face was free of makeup. He was glad she was pretty. He would hate to have been cooped up with some ugly hag for two days. He was kind of hoping she would soften up to him a bit though. Maybe give them something to do to while away the hours until Clayton showed up. But it didn't look like it was going to happen that way.

"Exactly what won't I get away with?" he asked, amused.

"Kidnapping, for one. Then there's black mail, assault with a deadly weapon, and whatever else you've resorted to in the last two weeks."

George laughed and went on eating. "Who's going to be around to say anything?"

Kelly's eyes widened and a cold shaft of fear plunged into her stomach. So far he had been decent to her, giving her hope that he would continue to be. But now she didn't know.

"Are you going to kill me?" she asked weakly.

He stared at her while he chewed his food, enjoying the fact that she was afraid of him. Maybe he should just leave it that way. Keep her afraid. That's the way he'd always liked women. Only Virginia had been different from all the others. Maybe that was why he'd been scared to leave her for all these years.

Instead of answering Kelly's question, he went back to eating. With sagging spirits Kelly turned her gaze dejectedly toward the busy harbor.

Bill closed his briefcase after the airport security official had examined it thoroughly. He walked down the concourse and joined Jake in the waiting room for the flight to Hong Kong.

"I've been thinking about the best way to deal with this," Jake said after Bill sat down beside him. "When we get there, you should call George. Ask to speak to Kelly. You've got to find out if she's okay."

"You mean alive," Bill said between clenched teeth.

Jake cleared his throat. "Yeah."

Bill squeezed his eyes shut in an effort to close out all thoughts of what could have happened to Kelly.

He had been such a fool all along with her. She was the first person who had ever come into his life and made him feel worthwhile, who made him want to share all that he was or ever would be.

To so many, he was a success. But, in love, he'd been nothing but a failure. He had been afraid to love . . . until Kelly came along. Only now the chance to show her what she meant to him might have been taken away. He had to find her. She had to be all right. Life wouldn't finally give what he had always been waiting for and then snatch it away so callously!

Jake continued, forcing Bill's thoughts back to their mission. "What you want to do is to get George to release her before you give him the chip. Now, he probably won't do it, but that's what you want to try for, okay?"

"Right."

"What we'll do is wait in the lobby of the Regent. When the switch is made, you'll take Kelly away to someplace safe. I'll handle George."

Bill shot a glance at Jake, but said nothing. He had a score to settle with George, but so did Jake. And Bill's first responsibility was Kelly. He'd take care of Watterman later.

The two men sat quietly, working out all the details in their minds, running over every eventuality until they heard the call for their flight. Picking up the briefcase with the gam

258

chip inside, Bill and Jake boarded the eight o'clock flight for Hong Kong.

"He may not show, you know."

Kelly turned from her post by the window and glared again at George. "He'll show."

George leaned back in the chair by the desk, close enough to the phone to grab it before Kelly could if it should ring. "How long have you known Clayton?"

Kelly clenched her hands in front of her and thought about ignoring the question. "Two weeks," she answered begrudgingly.

"Ho, ho!" he laughed. "Then I think you're in for a big surprise, sweetheart. Clayton's liable to just leave you high and dry. Just like he has all the others."

She looked away.

"Oh, yeah," he grinned, delighting in making her squirm. It relieved his own tension to create some in her. Gave him the edge he needed right now. "I had old Bill Clayton checked out by some private detectives. Had to know what kind of man I was dealing with, you know. So I had a detailed profile drawn up on him. He had a daddy who was a real loser, a deadbeat. Couldn't find work, had no education. Had to get married cause he got Bill's mama pregnant."

At Kelly's startled expression, he nodded.

"Yep, you didn't know that about old Bill, did you? Been fighting that curse all his life. Seems he's so scared of being a loser like his daddy, he turned into some sort of crazed workaholic. Never had time for women. A real love 'em and leave 'em type."

Kelly stared at George as he related all of this with such casual glee. She didn't put too much stock in what he said. After all, George Watterman was a very sick man. Still, some of it made sense. Bill's fear of failure. His need for total control over his own life, his inability to get close to anyone and admit how much he needed another person.

It was very sad in a way. Maybe all along his tough-guy image had been a façade. Underneath was probably a scared, lost little boy desperately in need of security and love.

But would he discover that he needed her in time to help her? She didn't believe for a minute that Bill wasn't coming. He would come for her. He would!

She pressed her fist to her mouth and held back the small cry of anguish that begged to come out. She had to believe in him. She had to have hope. At this point she had nothing else left.

Bill placed the call from the lobby of the Regent. If anything had gone wrong, he wanted to be close by where he could get to Watterman's room quickly. Jake was at the circular check-in desk in the middle of the lobby trying to obtain George's room number. When he turned back around, he gave Bill a thumbs-up sign, then moved over to a small waiting area and sat down.

The phone was answered after one ring.

"Watterman?"

"Yep."

"Before anything else is said, I want you to put Kelly on the line."

The man simply laughed. "No way, Clayton. Just leave the briefcase at the desk and the name of the hotel where you're staying and I'll send the girl along later."

Bill paused, debating over the best possible course of action. "I won't do it," he said. "I'll leave the case, but only if you send her down here now."

"You must not want to see this little lady very badly."

Bill squeezed the receiver so hard his knuckles were white. "Send her down, Watterman. I'll leave the chip and I'll wait out in front of the hotel. But if I see you come down to get it, and she's not there, I'm coming in after you."

"Leave it now, Clayton. And this time it better be the right chip. I know now how to identify it, and I won't let the girl go until I know it's the right one."

Bill paused for a minute before agreeing. "Okay, but, Watterman? She sure as hell better not have a single fingerprint of yours on her, or you're a dead man."

Bill hung up the phone. The game plan was set. All he could do now was wait. But first he dropped the package off at the front desk and watched the clerk switch on George's message light. He walked over to the seating area and Jake stood up.

"Well . . ." Bill stretched out his hand. "I guess this is it."

Jake fumbled with the cigar in his mouth but didn't yet light it. He held out his hand to meet Bill's. "Yeah, looks that way."

"What will you do after this?"

Jake narrowed his dark eyes in thought and removed the cigar from his mouth. "I've got some old friends in Palermo I haven't seen in, oh, a hundred years or so. Think I'll go look them up."

"Well, you take care of yourself, Balletoni."

"Yeah, you, too, Clayton."

"Maybe we'll meet again some—" He paused and looked around the lobby self-consciously, unaccustomed to such feelings. He shoved his hands into his pockets. "Well, ciao."

"Ciao."

Bill turned and walked through the front doors of the lobby. He stood just outside, waiting . . . waiting for whatever would happen next.

Kelly watched every move George made. She knew it had been Bill on the phone and she wished there were some way she could have made a noise or something to let him know she was all right. But George had his revolver pointed right at her and she was afraid even to breathe.

The message light had flashed on and she knew that everything was going to move a little faster now.

But she just had no idea how quickly!

As soon as the light came on, George leaped from his chair and grabbed her arm. "We're going downstairs now and you will stick right by my side. You got that?"

"Yes." She was so frightened, it took tremendous force to get that one word out.

"Let's go then."

George pulled Kelly down the hallway to the elevator and then down to the first floor.

From then on everything moved in fast motion. George's attention was riveted on the chip that was waiting for him at the desk and Kelly saw her chance to break away. As he asked for the package and took it from the desk clerk, Kelly wrenched free from his grasp and ran for the exit. She didn't look back to see if he was following her. And she closed off all thoughts of the gun that might be pointed at her back at this very moment. She never slowed her stride.

Once outside, she kept running down the driveway toward the main road. She heard someone shouting behind her, but she ignored it. Nothing was going to stop her now.

"Kelly!"

The sound kept getting closer until finally the timbre of that voice and the touch of that hand on her arm penetrated the block of fear in her brain. Bill grabbed her arm, pulling her into his embrace. The tears began to fall.

CHAPTER SEVENTEEN

Bill opened the door of his hotel room for Kelly to enter first. After he closed the door he did nothing but stare at her for a long time. It was as if he were seeing her for the first time ever. Her hair was windblown and her face was bare of makeup, but she had never looked more beautiful to him. No one had ever looked more beautiful.

In slow motion they reached for each other, expressing all their worry, doubts, hopes, and love in one embrace. "Kelly." The single word was expended in a sigh of gratitude.

She planted small kisses across his chest, standing on tiptoe to reach under his chin. Her breath was warm against his neck, her lips moist and generous. "You mean you were actually worried about me?" she breathed against his skin.

Bill leaned back, holding her arms in his huge grasp. "Are you kidding! Ruin this great tour worrying about some dizzy broad?"

She laughed and struck his chest with her fist.

He pulled her back into his tight embrace. "On the other hand, everybody needs a dizzy broad to fret over."

"You fretted?" she asked weakly, absorbing the scent of his skin, the strength of his arms around her.

"Endlessly."

"Good." She sighed, tasting the salty skin of his neck. "I hope you lost ten pounds because you couldn't eat. I hope your eyes are bloodshot because you couldn't sleep. I hope—"

"Let's not get carried away," he whispered against her ear. His fingers slithered up her side and slipped between their bodies, covering and tantalizing her breasts with each slow stroke.

She moaned softly in the V of his shirt and whispered, "Oh, but let's do get carried away."

Dropping down to slip an arm beneath her knees and another under her arms, Bill scooped her up against him and carried her to the king-size bed. While he walked slowly toward it, her fingers wove through the shimmering strands of his hair and her eyes looked deeply into his.

He sat on the bed, holding her in his lap. His large slow hand ran down her side to rest on her hip. "Do you want to know what I thought about while you were away from me?"

His eyes gleamed with a heat that sent wild impulses catapulting through her stomach. She could only nod.

"I thought about your laughing eyes, so soft and gray and honest." He ran a finger across the lids of each and she closed them to receive his gentle kiss. She opened them again only when he pulled back.

He lifted one of her hands and spread her fingers apart. "I thought a lot about these." He kissed each one and ran his tongue between them. "And how good it feels when you touch me." He placed her hand against his chest, and her fingers eagerly began to work at his shirt buttons.

He eased her back gently on the bed while her hand continued its journey down the front of his shirt. When she reached his waist, she pulled the shirttail from beneath the waistband of his jeans. Her hands spread across the expanse of his chest, electrifying his nerves wherever they were touched.

He stared at her parted lips. She flicked her tongue out, leaving the bottom lip wet and waiting. "I thought constantly about your mouth," he said, lowering himself over her. "I went crazy thinking about how it felt against mine, how you taste so warm, so good." He touched her lips lightly, his tongue darting out to circle the fleshy outline.

His tongue dipped inside her mouth, seeking out the memory, tasting it, savoring it, loving it. "Just as I remembered," he murmured against her neck, gliding his tongue down to the top button of her dress. "Just as I remembered."

With agonizing slowness he eased each button through its hole, stopping at the waist only long enough to untie her sash before continuing his descent with the buttons below her waist. When he reached the last one he spread her dress apart and his heated gaze touched every square inch of exposed skin.

His fingers rose to the lacy white bra and in one deft movement, flicked the front clasp open. It, too, fell to the sides of her body, laying bare the breasts that ached for his touch again.

One finger snaked out to swirl the tip of one soft mound. He moved to the other, teasing her with the same seductive leisure. "Maybe you didn't think about me too much," he grinned as her eyes fell closed.

She opened them slowly, lazily wanting his hands to go on forever in their teasing caresses. "Never," she smiled, reaching up to pull him down to her.

Their mouths met again, each pulling all the sweet yearning from the other. "Liar," he groaned, sliding his hardened body along the tensing fibers of hers. He dropped down, his mouth slipping over the angle of her chin, wandering down her neck and onto her breast. His tongue circled as slowly and teasingly as his finger had only a moment before. But the fire that burst into flame beneath his tongue was more intense and more alive than anything she had ever felt before.

She loved the feel of his body, hard with desire, on top of her, his slow, grinding movements as he pressed her farther into the mattress. And his voice, like warm, slow honey flowing against her neck.

"I thought of this every moment. I thought of kissing you everywhere, wanting you so badly, I was afraid I would explode."

He pushed his body back up, his hardened maleness pressing into her, his hands on each side of her head, his face only inches from hers. "I worried about you, Kelly. I was sick with worry. I ached for you."

Her hands clasped his hips and kneaded the flesh beneath his slacks, urging him closer, closer, wanting to feel the throbbing heat deep within her.

"How long are you going to make me wait?" She nipped his chin between her teeth. "How long?"

His answer was to shift higher, grinding even harder against her while he watched the play of passion unfold across her face. He moved against her rhythmically, smiling when she moved against him.

"You deserve it . . . for all the torture you've put me through." He finally sat up, pulling her with him. "Don't you know what I've gone through since I met you?" he asked, gently pushing her back down on the bed.

Her head arched back when his hand closed over her breast, then inched its way down her abdomen. His finger dipped beneath the edge of her panties and stroked back and forth. "Tell me," she breathed.

He stood up and pulled her dress the rest of the way off. Ever so slowly, he slid her panties down past her ankles, then yanked his shirt off his shoulders.

His fingers loosened his belt. "Let me count

the ways," he said, dropping his pants to the floor.

His mouth moved not down her body, but up it, starting at her ankles and climbing in a long, sensual trail up her calves, over her knees, along the insides of her thighs. His tongue stroked her until she gasped. Looking up at her face, he knew he could not torture either of them any longer.

So he moved into her with slow, hot strokes that filled her and wrapped him in a cloak of ecstasy. "Don't ever leave me again, Kelly. I need you." His breath grew shorter, more rapid with each passing second.

She matched him breath for breath, stroke for stroke, while his words poured over her in a rush of love. He needed her! He really wanted her! What more could she want or expect from this man? His next words came to her in a blinding rush, a deafening crescendo. "I love you, Kelly. I love you." She plunged into the flaming depths as he followed her and the two of them clung to each other in the pulsating ride.

A long time later they still lay wrapped in the warmth and security of each other's arms. The ships in the harbor moved back and forth from one port to another outside the window of their hotel.

"I meant what I said, Kelly. I love you so

much. I never even imagined that I could feel like this. I've been floundering for so long and I never even knew why. Does that make sense?"

Kelly ran her hand down the hard length of his chest. "All the sense in the world."

The streets in Wanchai were nothing like Jake remembered them. It was in the fifties when he was first here and it had been in the late sixties when he last saw the world of Suzie Wong in all its glory, when American servicemen from Vietnam overflowed the bars, spilling out into the streets. Now the nightclub strip was nothing more than a shadow of what it had once been. Still it had its own special flavor. Clubs with names like Pussycat and Wild Horse still lit up the sidewalks at night. Dai pai dongs, the small food stalls, lined the streets, emitting a flavor all their own.

But Jake didn't have time to stop and savor any of it right now. George Watterman had left the Regent immediately after he received the chip. He walked to the Star ferry and rode it from Kowloon to Hong Kong. Docking at the pier on the island, he had then taken a taxi down Queen's Road East into the Wanchai district. Jake had been behind him the whole way.

Now, as they walked through the famous

red-light district, Jake kept his distance while still keeping a careful eye on George.

George stopped and pulled a small piece of paper from his pocket and studied it for a moment. He turned left and entered a narrow alley between a theater and an exotic dance club that led from Wanchai Road to Cross Street. Jake watched him enter the empty alley. If he was going to confront him, he couldn't pass up this opportunity.

"George!"

The man in front of him stopped, his shoulders snapping to attention as he turned around, disbelief etched in the age lines in his face. George's tongue flicked out to lick his thick lips and he nodded. "Jake."

Jake walked closer, slowly but without any fear. "You got the chip?" he asked quietly.

"Yes." George's body was rigid and wary as he watched Jake move a few steps closer.

"Maybe we should talk about this, George. After all, we've been together a long time."

"Nothing to talk about anymore, old friend." His voice sounded tired and each syllable had a slow, drawn-out slur.

"I don't believe that," Jake said. "We've always been able to talk."

"Not anymore."

"Why?"

"Times change."

273

"Not all that much, George. We're still the same."

George pursed his lips and looked at the stone wall beside him, contemplating where his life had gone and why. "I've made some bad financial moves," he finally said, looking back at Jake.

"Haven't we all. But you don't want to do anything foolish."

"You wouldn't understand, Jake. You've always been a nobody. You came from some rathole in the Mediterranean and that's where you'll end up."

There was a moment of tense silence as the words echoed around him.

"Without me you'd be a nobody still," George added bitterly.

"And what are you now, George?" Jake asked. "What has all this made you?"

"I'm going to retire rich. I'm going to leave the company as a success. I pulled myself up by the bootstraps. I worked myself to the top. Nobody's going to take that from me."

"I didn't know anyone was planning to," Jake said.

"The company's been in trouble for a long time. I've been in trouble too. Virginia spend my money like it's going out of style. Only there's nothing left to spend. It's all gone. A of it."

"And this chip is your ticket to a comfort-able retirement?"

"I don't have much longer, Jake. My heart, my money . . . hell, it's all petered out. It's not my retirement. It's my life. It's what I've worked for since I was a kid. I'm not going to let it all go to hell."

"Who are you dealing with?"

"I've sold it to a toy company. Millions, Jake. It's worth millions."

Jake stared at him for a long moment, aware of a withering inside. "You used me, you bastard."

George laughed. "I've always used you. And you've used me. We all use each other every day. But hell, Jake. We were friends too."

"That's something you can't trade on, George."

George shrugged.

"Was it worth wasting Dawson and Klein-man?" Jake asked. "Oh, yeah, I know about that," he added at George's surprised look. "Was it worth kidnapping the Milburn girl? I hope to hell you didn't hurt her, because, take my word for it, Clayton will come after you. And he's a mean son of a bitch.

Jake stared at his old friend for a long mo-ment, wondering. They had been through so much together, seen it all, it seemed. Is this

275

what it all came down to in the end? He chuckled a bit wistfully at a long-ago memory. "Remember that time we had that dune buggy race with those sheiks from Abu Dhabi?"

George nodded. "Nineteen sixty-four."

"Yeah, that's right," Jake mused. "For us it was just a game, remember? But for those guys it was their lives."

"And you convinced me to let them win."

"But don't you see, George, they had to. It came down to honor in the end." Jake paused and looked directly at George. "Was all of this worth . . . your honor?"

"It was worth it," George said. "You've always had a hangup about that honor crap."

"Yeah, maybe I have."

George's eyes wavered a little, and a muscle in his jaw jumped erratically. "Come with me, Jake. You'll be a rich man for the rest of your life. For the old times . . . don't stop me."

"I can't let you do it, George. Call it honor if you want. Whatever it is, I can't let you do it to the company or to yourself . . . or to me. I won't. I want you to give me the chip."

For the first time since he heard Jake behind him in the alley, George looked down at Jake's hand. It was thrust into the pocket of his leather jacket and there was the hint of a protrusion pushing against the material.

276

"What are you going to do, run me in?" George laughed.

Jake shook his head. "No. I'm not a cop. What you do now is up to you. All I want is to take the chip back to the company. That's what I was hired to do."

"I don't have anything to lose if you kill me. But I have everything to lose if I give you the chip."

"But what you don't seem to realize, George, is that you've already lost. You can't sink any lower."

George swallowed hard and licked his lips. He felt the quickening pace in his heart and his chest began to tighten like a piece of leather stretched across a drum.

Jake didn't move a muscle. "A dark alley in Hong Kong. Not much honor in dying here, George."

The pump inside of him began to beat faster and harder. He didn't have his pills with him. He'd left them in the hotel room. He could draw his gun and try to take Jake, but there was no way he could be fast enough.

"Slow and easy now," Jake said as he watched George open the flap of his coat, reach in, and pull out the ceramic case. He tossed it, sending it skimming across the concrete to land at Jake's feet. Jake picked it up and flipped it over between his fingers. He looked up at George, mistaking the pale complexion and tight lips for signs of defeat. "You coming with me?"

George shook his head. He didn't trust his voice not to betray the pain that was ripping through him.

"Okay," Jake said slowly. "Okay." Sparing them both the indignity of useless farewells, he turned and left the alley, following the route he had taken before, only this time he didn't cross the harbor. He went straight to his hotel to collect his bag, and headed for the airport.

For several long minutes after Jake had gone, George stayed in the alley, slumped over with pain, unable to move. He had to get to the hotel, get to his pills. Then he could think about what to do next. Maybe he could catch up to Jake, change his mind. Maybe Finally, using all of his will, he managed to stumble out to the street.

It took quite a while for the sight of his unconscious body on the ground to pique the interest of a passerby. And by then it was much too late.

CHAPTER EIGHTEEN

Ms. Ruth Evanston
Managing Editor
Touring Magazine
111 Wacker Drive
Chicago, Illinois

Dear Ruth;

I am writing this as I sit in the Hong Kong airport waiting for the flight back to the States. There are two reasons for the letter. One, I am enclosing the article for *Touring Magazine*. The second reason is to let you know that I'm leaving the company. I can almost see your expression now, and I just hope you'll keep reading so that I can try to explain it all.

First of all, I realize now that it was a good idea not to send Calvin on this tour. It would have blown his mind. Digging for Ramepithicus in Tanzania is more his style. But I guess you knew that from the beginning.

I was separated from the tour for a couple of days, but . . . well, that's another story altogether. Now I'm waiting with the others for the flight home.

The flock remains together, but less tightly huddled now. We have our wings and have left the nest, so we no longer seem to need each other quite as much as we did in the beginning. We are confident enough to wander and explore a bit on our own, knowing that if we go too far Angel (he's our intrepid tour guide) will sweep us back into the fold with his ever widening wing.

The plane is due to board any minute but Lapito Ruta Migada Angelique is still trying to orchestrate every movemen with officious zeal. You will learn abou each of these people when you read m article, but this letter can serve as a post script for each of them.

At this moment Pearl Henshaw is giv

ing some sort of tongue-lashing to Mr. Fowler, our own personal G.I. Joe who has seen this whole tour as some sort of military campaign. I can't hear what she is saying, but all I can say is "It's about time somebody did it!"

Mrs. Willard finally woke up and realized we are now in Hong Kong. She's been asleep since we left New York two weeks ago. Her teenage niece, Muffy, seems uncommonly subdued at this moment and all I can guess is that she's out of chewing gum. Such sacrifices we Americans make when we travel!

The Parkers have finally tranquilized their children for the flight home. I wish I had told them to do that the first day. It doesn't really matter that much now because we're all so anesthetized to the little monsters at this point anyway.

Damien Brewster has given up trying to find the love of his life and is actually sitting in the waiting area reading Samuel Beckett. Such are the mysteries of life.

Winfred Rotterborg, still dressed as an aging representative for L. L. Bean, and Edna Blumberg, in pink polyester, seem to have hit it off very well and are now exchanging addresses.

But the biggest surprise of all is the Caldwells. The sweet little old couple who happily bought up half the Asian continent's supply of doodads is now being detained by customs officials. Apparently they have spent the last ten or fifteen years carrying merchandise into the States without declaring it. All these years they have been stocking their import-export shop back in Cincinnati with duty-free merchandise. Jonathan Evanston, our gay extra-terrestrial, has been traveling incognito as a professor from Iowa but is, in fact, a United States customs agent who has been trailing the Caldwells around the world. Boy, was ever fooled! He would probably have waited to arrest them when they tried to go through customs in the U.S. but, believe it or not, they actually walked up to Evanston and, because he had nothing of his own to take back to the States, they asked him to carry some of their stuff through so they wouldn't have to declare it. Talk about rotten luck!

It's funny how two weeks ago the thought of spending time with these people seemed like a fate worse than death I've learned a lot since then.

I have purposely saved one member of

the tour for last. Bill Clayton. It has to do with the second reason for this letter, the reason I will no longer be working for *Touring Magazine*. Hang on to your green pen, Ruth. Bill Clayton and I are getting married.

Remember how I said to you that nothing exciting ever happens on these tours? Well, I was wrong. In the last two weeks my whole life has changed. I've learned so much about myself and about what I want and need out of life. Though we come from distinctly different backgrounds, Bill Clayton and I are very much alike. Cut from the same mold, if you will. And more important than that, we need each other. Desperately.

I'll be going with him to Denver and very soon I will come back to Chicago for my things. I realize that this is hardly the fair way to quit my job. I don't want to leave you in a bind. But, for the first time in my life, I'm doing what is right for me. This is the only excitement I've ever really wanted.

Hope the article pleases you. I'll keep you informed on our wedding plans.

Sincerely,
Kelly

"All finished with the letter?" Bill watched Kelly stuff the envelope and seal it.

"All done. I'll mail it when we land in the States. What are you reading there?"

Bill opened the airline magazine to the section on gifts. "I was just looking at this Atari contraption. Think I'll give this to you for a wedding present."

She cocked her head and smiled coyly at him. "I can think of plenty of other games I'd rather play—games you play in the night."

He tossed the magazine down on the floor and placed an arm on the back of her chair. "Oh, yeah? Like what?"

"Wouldn't you like to know," she teased.

He leaned closer. "I have to tell you, I'm not a very good loser. So if you intend on winning all the time . . ."

She rested a hand on the back of his neck. "I don't think you'll mind losing the games I have in mind."

"Hmm. Are these games long and involved?" he whispered near her ear.

"Never-ending," she said.

He expelled a quick breath and shook his head, amazed at his own good fortune. "I may become a real game addict myself. Of course you'll have to teach me all the different maneuvers that you know."

She smiled and ran a slow finger down into the collar of his shirt. "Stick with me, kiddo, and you'll learn it all."

*LOOK FOR NEXT MONTH'S
CANDLELIGHT ECSTASY SUPREMES*